After every tough climb to the top, there's a descent. Sometimes, it's real easy, just a matter of sliding down feet first. Other times, it's like a tumble off a steep cliff – with a hell of a lot of rocks. Nobody ever promised downhill would be a piece of cake. Have fun with that.

Other Books By C.M. Stunich

The Seven Wicked Series
First
Second
Third
Fourth
Fifth
Sixth
Seventh

Hard Rock Roots
Real Ugly
Get Bent
Tough Luck
Bad Day
Born Wrong
Dead Serious
Doll Face
Heart Broke
Get Hitched

Houses Novels
The House of Gray and Graves
The House of Hands and Hearts and Hair
The House of Sticks and Bones

The Huntswomen Trilogy
The Feed
The Hunt
The Throne

Indigo Lewis Novels

Indigo & Iris
Indigo & The Colonel
Indigo & Lynx

Never Say Never Trilogy & Never Too Late Series
Tasting Never
Finding Never
Keeping Never
Tasting, Finding, Keeping: The Story of Never (omnibus)
Never Can Tell
Never Let Go
Never Did Say

Triple M Series
Losing Me, Finding You
Loving Me, Trusting You
Needing Me, Wanting You
Craving Me, Desiring You

A Duet
Paint Me Beautiful
Color Me Pretty

Stand Alone Novels
She Lies Twisted
Hell Inc.
A Werewolf Christmas (A Short Story)
Fuck Valentine's Day (A Short Story)
DeadBorn
Broken Pasts
Crushing Summer
Taboo Unchained
Taming Her Boss

Clan of the Griffin Riders
Chryer's Crest
Brixus' Battle

C.M. STUNICH

Doll Face
Copyright © C.M. Stunich 2014

All rights reserved. Printed in the United States of America. No part of this book may be used or reproduced in any manner whatsoever without written permission except in the case of brief quotations embodied in critical articles or reviews. For information address Sarian Royal Indie Publishing, 1863 Pioneer Pkwy. E Ste. 203, Springfield, OR 97477-3907.
www.sarianroyal.com

ISBN-10: 1938623827 (pbk.)
ISBN-13: 978-1-938623-82-0(pbk.)

Optimus Princeps font © Manfred Klein
"El&Font Gohtic!" Font © Jérôme Delage
Cover art and design © Amanda Carroll and Sarian Royal

The characters and events portrayed in this book are fictitious. Any similarity to real persons, living or dead, businesses, or locales is coincidental and is not intended by the author.

to the growling whispers of unsung voices, may your words be heard and your ire soothed.

this book is dedicated to the lost, the broken, and the bleeding. may you find your own song.

*Author's Note:You know that feeling you get right after you sit down on a roller coaster? The one you get after waiting in the hot sun for an hour, working up your bravado and smiling at your friends to get past the butterflies in your stomach? Then you sit down in that hard seat, fasten that belt across your lap and wonder what the hell you just got yourself into. This book is kind of like that. Only worse. Enjoy! ~CM

"Hard Rock Roots" Reading Order:
Book #1: Real Ugly
Book #2: Get Bent
Book #3: Tough Luck
Book #4: Bad Day
Book #5: Born Wrong
Book #6: Dead Serious
Book #7: Doll Face
Book #8: Heart Broke

~CM

CHAPTER 1
LOLA SAINTS

Ten minutes earlier ...

Click.

Crap. I smack my gum and ignore the sound of a hammer being pulled back behind me. At this point in my life, I'm not even surprised. My fingers curl around the handgun in my bag.

"Poppet," I say, twisting my head to look at my sister. She seems surprised that I knew it was her, but I already saw her when I was onstage, standing at the front of the crowd and staring up at me. Maybe she thought the press of sweaty bodies gave her anonymity?

They didn't.

"Nice heels, babe," I tell her, my voice decidedly lackluster. Even discovering the spark in my life that is Ronnie fuckin' McGuire, I haven't been able to pull myself out of this funk. Thinking your sister's being held hostage is bloody terrifying. Finding out she's actually betrayed you is *heartbreaking*. It might sound selfish, but I think the fear was easier to deal with than the betrayal. I nod my chin at Poppet's orange heels and lift my eyes slowly to her face. Her blonde hair hangs loosely around her shoulders and her blue eyes are sparkling with an odd mixture of pain and frustration. I'm about to make a nasty comment about her ugly arse dye job, tell her that *brunette* was definitely a better look on her when I notice what's clutched in her left hand. Three times as fucked as the semi-automatic she's holding in her right, there's a Goddamn kid's T-shirt rumpled in her fingers – complete with ankle biter.

Fuck a nun's dry cunt.

"Oh, *shit*, Poppet," I growl, squeezing my gun tighter. If it were anyone else – Cohen, Honesty, KK – I would've already shot 'em. But ... Poppet is my sister. My *sister*. My brain swirls with happy memories as my heart weeps in frustrated pain. This is not how things were supposed to turn out. This bitch was supposed to be in fuckin'

France, living with her cheese making husband. It's not right, just ain't fuckin' right. "Who's the kid?"

"Doesn't matter, Lola," she tells me confidently. There's a sense of conviction in her voice that scares the shite out of me. It's the kind of confidence that only crazy people get, right before they jump off the deep end and drown. She shakes the poor boy around by his shirt and a few tears escape, rolling down his cheeks as he looks at me in terrified desperation. I would say I knew my sister, that she'd never hurt a child, but this woman in front of me with the bad bleach blonde hair and the dangerous eyes? She might as well be a stranger. "What matters right now is that you've got one more chance, *one* chance to redeem yourself." I rise to my feet, the sounds of Turner's and Naomi's voices blending into white noise around me. Poppet moves a step forward, keeping her gun trained on my chest, but she lets me keep my bag, doesn't even seem to notice I've got my hand all shoved up in it.

"Eh?" I lift an eyebrow and close my eyes, trying to decide exactly what it is here that's really important. I'm only going to have a split second to make a decision and once I do, that's it. "Redeem myself?" I open my eyes and find Ronnie looking back at me, mouth tight, hands shaking. Cohen Rose is standing next to him with a gun clutched in his grubby ass fingers. *No.* My heart picks up speed and slams into my ribcage, reverberating through my bones, liquifying them. I want to collapse to the floor, cover my head with my hands and scream. That dream I was chasin'? It's turned into a fucking nightmare. "How on earth do I go about doing *that,* Poppet? I was under the impression that I was one of the good guys." I wink at her and force a smile to my face. If Cohen looks this way and sees the fear in my eyes, he'll shoot Ronnie and that'll be the end of that. Where's that stupid Irish fuck, Brayden Ryker? I'll tell you what, that ginger haired bastard isn't worth his weight in salt. Even *I* knew shit was going to go down tonight. Fucking hell.

"Lola, this isn't about good versus evil. There's no such thing. It's just about us versus them. You're either *with* us or you're *with* them. When I first met Stephen, you were firmly entrenched in *us*. But now? Now, I don't know what to think." Poppet swallows and yanks the kid closer. I don't know how old he is – six? seven, maybe? – but it doesn't matter. The fear in his eyes is hard to miss. I examine my sister's round face, letting my gaze sneak past her to catch on Ronnie. Cohen's got him and Jesse pinned against a wall now. Ronnie's brown eyes are still focused on me, his muscles tight with barely leashed violence. If I don't act now, he will. He'll risk

everything to save me, I know that.

Oh God.

I close my eyes again and force myself to breathe. I love Ronnie. I do. I've been scared to admit that to myself because, bloody fuck, who falls in love this fast? But it's true. That's why I couldn't do what Stephen wanted me to do. I couldn't drive Ronnie into the dirt, crush his soul, break him. And I can't be a part of Poppet's madness, not even if I love her, too. I have to make a choice *now*. This kid in front of me, he hasn't done anything wrong. And Ronnie? He's got so much to live for. Friends that are really family, parents that love him, kids that are gonna need him.

If I really think about it, the decision's easy to make.

"I love you huge, babe," I tell Poppet, opening my eyes back up and staring into hers. They're blue, just like mine, like the sea of the Gold Coast on a bright day. I force my lips to keep smiling as I grip the revolver inside the bag and make myself think about our last vacation there, when we were still in secondary school, when we stayed in a room on the thirtieth floor and sat on the patio painting each other's nails. If I'm going to die on this tour like I always suspected I might, it's going to be with fucking happy memories spinnin' round my skull. I pull

up Ronnie's face, smiling down at me, his hand brushing my hair back, the feeling of his body inside mine. Poppet gives me a strange look as the bag slides to the floor between us.

She sees the gun and starts to say something, but I'm not looking at her, I'm looking past her at Joel, Ice and Glass' guitarist, with his shaved head and rapturous gaze. He's next to Cohen, yelling something, screaming who the fuck knows what. Everything seems to be moving in slow motion around me. Maybe this is what happens when you find out you're gonna die? Time slows because you ain't got much of it left, giving you a split second to lay out all your regrets, say your prayers, realize that you'll never again kiss the lips of the man you love.

Joel is next to Cohen, and even though I'd *love* to put a bullet through my ex's skull, I think Joel is more dangerous. He loves Stephen like a God, and he's not as much of a coward as the big fat chode standing next to him. If anybody's going to follow orders and actually put bullets through brains, it's Joel.

I lift up my revolver, right over Poppet's shoulder and I fire.

The bullet hits Joel right in the chest, splatters blood across the wall behind him and drops him straight to his

knees. I shift my aim and take another shot at Cohen, but I don't have the luxury of seeing it strike flesh.

Pain blooms down below and my gaze moves back to Poppet as my arms collapse at my sides, as the revolver hits the floor, as my knees finally do collapse. My sister mouths something at me, but I can't hear what she says. My left hand touches my belly and comes away with thick redness. *Blood.*

But that's okay.

I smile because I deserve this. Because I've done things that can't be forgiven. I killed a girl that didn't deserve to die, played my part in the deaths of Ronnie's children's mothers. I fell in love too late, fucked up too damn much, and managed to help give Indecency a fighting chance.

Guess this is as good a way to go as any.

CHAPTER 2
Ronnie McGuire

Five minutes earlier ...

"LOLA!"

The scream that tears from my throat is fucking epic.

No.

No.

No fucking way.

"Lola!" I rise to my feet and slam into Cohen Rose, knocking him to his ass while he flails around and gapes like a fish out of water. I should probably stop and take

the gun from his fingers, knock his ass out, but I can't think of anything but Lola Saints.

The love of my life has just fallen to her knees with blood flowering across the front of her white tank top, the one that says *You're Never Naked When You're Wearing Ink*. The words are obscured by the sudden rush of red as Lola touches a hand to her belly and blinks her eyes several times in shocked surprise. The makeup running down her face might've started with the sweat she shed onstage, but now it's mixed with tears.

Lola's sister draws her weapon back and stumbles, like even she's having a hard time realizing what she's just done. The kid she dragged back here by the shirt looks heartbreakingly familiar. *Travis.* I would bet my balls that this boy is the son America told Turner and Naomi about, the son I learned only a few hours earlier actually existed. Turner told me that shit in a *text* on his way here. Not the kind of information you want rammed into your brain via electronics, but whatever. Who gives a shit about that, especially right now. I want to help the kid, I do, but I can't lose Lola. I can't. If I do, we both die. Everything falls apart. I was willing to sacrifice myself for her, but never in a million years did I think she'd sacrifice herself for me.

She loves me.

Wish I could be happy about that emotion. But if to learn about it, I have to say good bye, I'd rather not have known.

"Lola!" I collapse to the floor by her side and take her into my arms. There's so much going on around me, but as soon as my hands touch her skin, it all fades away. Chaos erupts around us like a volcano – spewing magma laden shit all over everything. One minute, I'm standing there with a water bottle in my hand, getting ready to take a peep out the curtains at Turner, the next there's a gun to my head. One pointed at Lola.

Poppet stumbles away, adjusting a wireless headset that she got from God only knows where. *Fuck, fuck, fuck.* I hold Lola in my trembling arms, digging my cell from my pocket while trying desperately not to jostle her. Shit is going down, and I'm torn between holding the girl I love and protecting my friends. *FUCK!*

"Ronnie," Lola whispers, her voice laced with terror as she grabs onto either side of my face. "What happens when I die? Do I go to hell for the things I've done?" Her nails scrape the skin from my cheeks as I dial 911 with my right hand and hold her as gently as I can with the other. A quick glance up shows me that Poppet's disappeared through the curtains. A split second later, the music stops and I can hear her voice booming through the

speakers.

"If you shoot him, then I'll shoot your son. I swear to God I'll do it."

"I don't know, doll face," I tell her, trying my best to smile. The 911 operator's talking in my ear, but I don't care. She can fucking wait. "But I can promise you that wherever it is, you're not going to find out until much, much later. You're gonna be okay. You are." Lola shakes her head as I look away and pinch my eyes closed, letting my voice turn mechanical as I try to report what's just happened to the operator. *Uh, a big fucking conspiracy has just crashed down on our heads. You should already have cops here doing crowd control, but I don't see them. Brayden Ryker is going to fucking die when I get my hands around his neck.*

A hand wrenches my phone from my fingers and drops it to the floor, crunching it under a pair of heavy boots. I glance up to find the man in question standing there with a frown on his face.

"What the FUCK?!" I scream at Brayden, but he's already moving away from us, leaving Lola there to bleed out on the floor. The man's face is a mask of professional hatred and deep-seated frustration. The look's enough to tell me that however it is that he got himself embroiled in this shit, it's personal.

"Ronnie, I'm going to die. And I deserve it, so it's okay. It's really okay," Lola whispers while Poppet's voice echoes through the speakers again, but I don't give a shit about what she's saying. It doesn't matter. Nothing matters except this.

"Lola, baby, you're *not* going to die." I try not to grit my teeth while I say it, but I can't help myself. Memories of Asuka are assaulting me from all angles. Her voice is reverberating in my skull and a scream rests on the tip of my tongue, a cry of outrage and pain that I'm afraid I won't be able to hold back much longer. But I have to. I have to stay strong for Lola. More gunshots ring out and my heart seizes. Turner and Jesse. They're my brothers and if they go, I go. And Naomi. If *she* goes, Turner goes. We're all connected here by the threads of fate, connected by a glistening web of heartstrings. One snaps, we bleed out collectively. Nice how the strongest emotion on earth can also become a weakness when put into the wrong hands. "I'm going to get you through this, okay?" I tell her, struggling to tear my shirt from my shoulders without jostling her body. Once I get the fabric free, I press it against the wound, trying to staunch the bleeding as best I can. I don't know why Brayden Ryker crushed my cell, but I'm damn sure I have to get Lola

some medical attention or she really will die here in my arms.

A hand slides across the floor next to us, diving for something ... *Lola's fucking gun.* My body tenses, but I can't push Lola aside and fight for it, so I clutch her tight and glance up sharply to find Trey's sister, Sydney, whipping the revolver around and pointing it at someone behind us.

"Back the fuck off!" she snaps, panting heavily, eyes focused on something I can't see.

"Go help your friends, love," Lola breathes, closing her eyes and reclining into my arms like she doesn't even have the will to fight.

"Goddamn it, Lola," I growl at her, snapping her out of her trance. "Wake the fuck up and stay with me. We'll get through this together." I can see that cursing at her's not doing me much good, so I switch tactics. "If you die, I die. I will seriously walk out of this building, find a knife and slit my own throat. Lola, I've already lost a soul mate and a brother. I barely survived it. If you leave me, too, that'll be the end, baby. Game over for Ronnie McGuire." I brush her hair back as she sets her lips in a thin line and curls her fingers around my arm. Maybe, just maybe, the strength and determination I know she has inside of her will buy us a few more minutes. "Sydney," I shout, hating how immobile I am. I *want* to get up, but I can't. Truth comes down to this: *nothing* here is more important to me than this woman. If I were to put her down and she died while I was somewhere else, my soul would be irreparably damaged, so fucked up that even if I were lucky enough to get reborn, I'd still be sad-sack Ronnie McGuire.

"Yep?" she asks, her voice rough and shaken. When she slipped her guest pass on and jumped in the van with us, I doubt she expected all of *this*.

"I need an ambulance for Lola, but Brayden fucked my phone up. Can you get out of here? Find a way to contact 911?" Sydney grunts in response as footsteps scatter around us, more shouts, another gunshot, and then another. The crowd explodes from beyond the curtain, bursting like a blister. I can hear the screaming, and I can just imagine the flailing stampede that it'll become. Within seconds, the death toll out there could reach astronomical levels. Don't believe me? At a concert for *The Who* in 1979, the doors weren't even opened yet, but the crowd heard the band's warm-up from outside and rushed the entrance thinking the concert was getting started without them. They managed to crush eleven people to death. Eleven people because they *thought* the

band was starting the concert. Here? There's a crazy woman on the speakers, gunshots, a history of violent excitement surrounding our band's tour.

What's eleven times like fucking infinity?

Shit.

"Lola," I say, feeling a few tears leak down my cheeks. She looks up at me from that beautiful round face of hers while crimson heat oozes out around my fingers, soaking through the shirt and dripping onto my jeans, pooling on the floor. Her lips are gently parted and her face is pale, so pale, ghostly white. *No, no, no, no.* I swallow hard, trying to get control of myself.

"LOS ANGELES!" It's a scream twice as epic as my own. *Turner Campbell.* "CALM THE FUCK DOWN!" The sound echoes around us all, smashing into my brain, paralyzing me even though I'm not fucking moving. *Thank God.* "Nobody's going to shoot you!" Turner sobs. Yes, sobs. You heard me. Freaking sobs. *Oh my God, Naomi Knox, NO.* "But if you don't calm down, you'll kill each other. You'll kill Naomi Knox. We need a doctor up here. Get on your phones, call 911. Somebody please. There has to be a fucking doctor out there."

My heart breaks for my friend and the crowd responds in turn, the raucous roar quieting to an equally intense murmur. A split second later, Brayden Ryker is bursting back through the curtains with blood on his boots and an angry scowl stuck to his lips.

"Don't tell the cops a feckin' thing," he snaps at me, sweeping by, acting as if the sight of Lola's broken body means friggin' nothing to him. "Not a Goddamn feckin' thing."

"Ronnie." It's Sydney, moving back around me and kneeling by my side. When she reaches out a hand and brushes it across my cheek, I know things are bad. I hug Lola tighter, and she grunts, forcing me to relax my grip. Our eyes meet again as Sydney speaks. "Help's on the way. I called 911." She glances back and cringes at something, presumably Brayden or one of his men, dropping her voice to a whisper. "I have no idea what just happened here, but if I were you, I'd keep my mouth shut. Don't say a word about what happened, not even about who shot Lola." Sydney stands up at the same moment I hear pounding footsteps. "He's dead," she calls out, and I hope she's referring to that bald guy Lola shot. If it's Jesse, I ... or even Milo. *Fuck.* "We need help over here."

"You're going to be okay," I promise Lola as they drag her from my arms and try to inspect me for injuries. I bat away gloved hands and ignore mechanically asked

questions as I try my best to keep my eyes on the love of my life. They load her up on a stretcher and carry her away, asking me if I'm family, taking my silence to mean *no*. At the last second, I tell them yes, but they're holding me back, and I think I'm screaming. I'm screaming and reaching for Lola, and she's disappearing into the back of an ambulance that's driving away before I can reach it.

I run after it for a long time, too long, until I hear cops screaming at me to stop.

When I do, I collapse to my knees and wonder how everything in my life has gotten so fucked up.

Dunno, dunno, dunno.

That's what I told the cops.

Dunno, dunno, DO NOT FUCKING KNOW.

I rock back and forth, head clutched in my hands as I try to force myself to breathe. Two feet away from me, Turner Campbell wails. No joke. Kid you not. Think he's a pussy for crying? Then you've never lost a loved one. Go fuck yourself.

"Turner!" Milo's trying desperately to get his attention, shaking his shoulder, grabbing his arm, even slapping the side of his face. It's a gentle Milo sort of a slap, but a slap nonetheless. Under normal circumstances, Turner would be slapping – or probably punching – him right back. "Turner Campbell." No response. Turner is sobbing right now, and I don't blame him. Naomi got shot, too. Apparently while trying to save the kid, Tyler Rutledge, from Poppet. This, supposedly, happened about thirty seconds before Brayden Ryker stormed back there and shot the woman right in the face, splattered her blood all over Naomi as she passed out, collapsing on top of a dead woman. This calls for a royal bout of cursing.

"Fuck," I growl under my breath, jerking my hands away from my face. We're sitting in a hotel room, but only because Brayden's men won't let us sit at the hospital. That's right. At *gunpoint,* we were escorted back here. To be fair, they tried asking nice first, but Turner exploded on their asses and now, here we are. Sitting on the edge of one of two queen beds and freaking the fuck out. The cops questioned us before we even got to the hospital and then, Brayden's people took over.

DOLL FACE

Whatever the hell is going on, it goes deep because apparently, their rules trump the law. That's fucking scary. "Leave him alone, Milo," I snap because shit, Turner has no idea if Naomi's even still alive. She was – just barely – when they threw her in an ambulance after Lola left, but life can change in the blink of an eye. Turner and I both know that oh so well.

America Harding killed Travis.

I close my eyes and swallow back a lump of pain and fear.

It wasn't Stephen Hammergren that ran my best friend over with his car; it was Amatory Riot's manager. She killed my friend because he wanted his kid, because he was a better man than I was – than I am – and now he's gone. He's gone and his kid's been raised by a man willing to torture and kill people as part of some elaborate revenge plot against his ex-wife.

"Fuck." That's the only word I feel capable of speaking right now, the only thing that seems appropriate. I've been trying to wait for Turner to calm down a little, so I can ask for more details. All I know at this point are facts I've been fed from everybody else, from Jesse who's thankfully still alive. Josh. Milo.

Dead.

That's also an important distinction to make here. Who *didn't* make it through that concert is just about as important as who did.

Stephen. America. Joel, the bald dude. Poppet.

Four dead people, several injured.

Blair. Cohen Rose. Honesty, the bassist for Ice and Glass as well as their guitarist, Chris. KK, Lola's manager. And most important of all: Naomi and … Lola.

"Go away, Milo. Can't you fucking see he doesn't want to talk right now? Go get us something to eat, Jesus Christ." I grab a pillow and chuck it at my manager, not in a playful way either. It's just, I gotta throw something, so it might as well be something that *doesn't* kill the guy. My mind is spinning and the only thing I can think about besides the violent shit storm that just occurred, is meth. I want a hit so bad I can taste it. How else am I supposed to survive this? There are so many elements to what just happened that are liable to destroy my life.

Lola shot Joel. She killed him.

Prison for life, anybody?

Oh, and let's not forget that the girl my best friend fell in love with, Naomi, she shot someone, too. America. She fucking killed her. In front of a crowd with numbers

in the tens of thousands. Add that to the footage exploding across the Internet, taken on cell phones and captured by raucous media members, and you've got some serious, serious problems.

I can't think right now. I want to lie down and sleep until there's news about Lola. But I can't. I glance over at Turner who's shaking and staring into space like he's not even home anymore. I recognize the look, and I can't let it go on. I've *been* there, done that before. *Asuka, please God, help me through this, I need your strength.*

I slide off the edge of the bed as Milo retreats and scoot on my knees to sit beside my friend. I have to snap my fingers several times to get his attention.

"Turner," I whisper, knowing a scream won't work any better to break through that trance. "Hey. You in there, bro?" Nothing. Not even a blink. At least he's not screaming anymore. I get the pain, but I don't know if I can hold myself *and* him up at the same time if he keeps wailing like that. The sound cuts straight through my head and into my brain, eviscerating me from the inside out. "Turner Motherfucking Campbell, wake your ass up."

"Go away, Ronnie," he drawls, leaning back, smashing into the bed with a shudder. "Leave me the hell

alone." I watch as he curls in on himself and starts to shake. *Shit.* I rise to my feet and look around the room. It's just us in here, with two of Brayden's men. I don't know where Amatory Riot is – or anyone else for that matter. Jesse, Josh, Sydney. Milo says he's seen them, that they're okay, but it's kind of freaking me the fuck out. Why separate us all? Hell, why put Turner and me together? I don't get it.

I close my eyes and take a deep breath.

Lola. God. Even though I've showered, I can still feel the stain of her blood on my hands. The warmth of it. The consistency. And then, as if that wasn't enough to fuck with my addled brain, I start to think about Asuka. About her blood. I start imagining that I have the crimson color of both girls splattered on my hands.

I open my eyes and shake my hands out, trying to get a hold of myself.

"Turner," I repeat, grabbing his leg and trying to roll him over, away from the headboard and towards me. "HEY!" I shout and he startles, flipping up to his feet and slamming his palms into my chest.

"WHAT?!" he screeches, shoving me again. "WHAT THE FUCK DO YOU WANT FROM ME?!" I let him yell, getting at least some small thrill of pleasure from

watching Brayden's guards shift uncomfortably. I force myself to smile at my friend.

"You can still scream like nobody else," I say as he rolls his eyes and thrusts an arm across his nose, wiping away the tears like they were never there. I watch as he visibly tries to contain himself. Same thing happened when Travis died. Not the wailing, not really. I mean if he did that in private, I don't know, but this gathering of the spirit that he's attempting, I saw that happen. Thing is, it didn't really work. Turner ended up drowning himself in sex and drugs and alcohol. He never really recovered, not until Naomi Knox showed up. I've got to protect this man the way I didn't protect Travis. My heart shudders in pain. "And I'm pretty sure it was that raging screech of yours that saved Naomi's life," I say, trying to be optimistic. Ask any of my friends: optimism has not generally been my strong suit. But I'm trying to change here, trying to fight for something I had once and never thought I'd have again. *Love.* Fuck. *Let's just get through this, get Naomi and Lola out of the hospital, start the fuck over again.*

"Yeah? Well, it's also sold millions of records and scored me countless chicks." Turner sniffles and then looks away, pain flashing over his features like lightning, a jagged slash of brightness that hurts the eyes and promises bad things to come. "But none of that is even half as important as this."

I reach out and touch my friend's shoulder, giving it a squeeze that I know'll piss Turner off, but will also hopefully distract him. When he doesn't call me a flaming faggot and slap my hand away, I know he's even worse off than I thought.

"You saved her, Turner," I tell him, still keeping hold of that fragile thread of optimism. She could still die, sure, but until I know for sure Naomi's six feet under, I'm going to keep telling half-truths to my friend's puffy face. Turner Campbell doesn't look like a mega rock star badass right now, but like the boy who used to stumble from his mother's trailer, dripping blood across the dusty pavement, tears streaming down his face. You should've seen him the day she microwaved some of the crappy ass plastic McDonald's toys he used to cart around. They were all he had, other than that one-legged G.I. Joe of course. "Shit, who knows how many lives you saved? I could hear the crowd from backstage, bro. If you hadn't calmed them down, there'd be a dozen or more people out there just as upset or worse than you are right now."

"I don't care about any of them," he snarls back at me, but I know that isn't true. He cares, and he knows he did the right thing. Turner jerks away from me and stalks

over to Brayden's bodyguards. One of them jerks back the hammer on his revolver but leaves it sitting in his lap like a threat. Huh. It's going to take a hell of a lot more than a gun to deter Turner Campbell. "What I care about is that the love of my life, my *fiancée*," Turner says, stressing the word, "is lying bleeding in a hospital bed. I want a phone to call the hospital. Fuck, I want a *car*, so I can drive my ass over there. Hell, I'll even let you goons come with. Whaddaya say?" I turn and give Turner's back a raised brow. Fiancée, huh? Either he's just doing his usual posturing or something happened between the two of them last night after they disappeared. I glance up at the curtains, at the streaming shafts of light that penetrate the dirty fabric. This is no fancy ass, golden sheets, ass licking employees kind of hotel like we've been staying in. This place is a shit hole. I really don't care since it's kind of what I'm used to, but the light outside does remind me that *last night* is a relative term. Technically, that was the night *before* last when Turner disappeared.

"I think you should sit down and wait for Brayden," the man says, his plain-Jane face peering up at Turner with little interest. Since America's dead, where does that leave us with these assholes? Milo doesn't even know anything about our security detail. That blonde bitch handled everything. "That's about all I can say right now."

"At least look it up for me," Turner growls out, leaning towards the guy, close enough that he's making him nervous. "Google her ass. See if she's still alive."

"Sorry, no can do," the man says, letting his eyes drift from Turner to the hotel room door. A moment later, it swings open and Brayden Ryker himself storms in, dressed in baggy black work pants and a short sleeved shirt. He lets the door swing shut behind him and puts his hands on his hips, looking between Turner and me with a tight pursing of his lips.

"I'm sorry about the way that all went down," Brayden says as Turner spins to face him with a poisonous look spreading across his face. "It was never my intention to let it go this far."

"Oh, *aye*," Turner says, lifting up his hands in frustration as he imitates Brayden's Irish accent in a mocking tone of voice. "*It twasn't me fault. I guess I just lost some of me lucky charms.*" To his credit, the man doesn't react, moving his hands from his hips and folding them across his broad chest. The sleeve of floral tattoos he has stretching across his massive bicep is a little disconcerting, giving Brayden this soft edge that I

DOLL FACE

know is one hundred percent for show. Those green eyes, the tattoos, the accent that makes American girls curl their toes, it's all a front. I imagine if he wanted to, Brayden could snap Turner's neck in like a second.

"Are you done then?" Brayden asks as Turner sags, the hot air going out of him faster than a popped fucking balloon. "'cause if you are, I've got some good news for you." My friend's head snaps up as I take a step closer and fall into line beside him, mimicking Brayden's pose by crossing my arms over my chest. "Lola and Naomi are both alive." My friend's body begins to shake as I close my eyes and let out a stale breath I hadn't realized I was still holding. "Miss Saints has been moved out of surgery and is in stable condition." I open my eyes back up and meet Brayden's moss colored irises, running my tongue across my lower lip and fighting to keep my emotions to a minimum while I wait to hear about Naomi. "Miss Knox is still in surgery, so I can't report much beyond the fact that she's still breathing."

Turner groans like he's been punched in the stomach, stumbling over to the bed and sitting down hard, curling his torso over his knees as he struggles to breathe through the rush of emotion.

"You'll have to stay here for a while while I sort things out. If you want to leave, you're free to do so, but I can promise you that the police will be waiting. If you want me to sort this out, give me some time." I open my mouth to ask one of the hundred questions I have crouching inside my chest when Brayden shakes his head, just so, and turns away, leaving the room and letting us drown in the silence of our own confusion.

CHAPTER 3
❦ LOLA SAINTS ❦

I wake up with a start, tubes hooked into my arms, latched onto me like the sea creature that was plaguing my dreams. Fucking octopus, all bright orange and leering, with penises instead of tentacles. Fuck a Goddamn duck, that shit was bloody terrifying.

I reach up to start ripping needles from my skin when a woman's hand clamps over my wrist and draws my attention up to her face. I recognize this chick as one of Brayden's people, some Amazonian lady with too much muscle mass and small little titties. I jerk my arm from her hand and press it against my chest. *I'm still alive.* The emotion overwhelms me, crashing down on my head and making me dizzy. Or maybe that's the bullet wound that stupid scrag of a sister gave me.

"Glad to see you're awake," the woman says, her hair like shadow in the darkness of my hospital room. I look around, but there's nobody else here. No Ronnie McGuire. My stomach clenches with pain and sends a tightness to my throat that I have trouble breathing around. I reach a hand down to touch the area where the bullet hit me, but it's buried under the blankets and the hospital gown, under bandages, probably stitches. I have no idea because as of right now, I can't really feel the damn thing. *Must be all the morphine, huh?* I get shot and wake up fried. Can't say I'm complaining about the second part of the equation. "Do you remember what happened, Miss Saints?"

"Uh," I drone as I scope out the room. It's so empty and sterile, no fuckin' flowers or nothing. I must not have been out for all that long. Eh. And after all those sappy, end of the world thoughts? Fuck me runnin'. "I shot Joel," I begin and the woman hisses under her breath, drawing my gaze back to her strange ass eyes. Pale as the fucking vodka I spend half my days slamming. I wrinkle my nose.

"No. That is not what happened. When the police come in to question you, you'll tell them the truth." I

DOLL FACE

raise a brow at the weird chick with the butch cut hair and the creepy eyes.

"Listen up there, twat-waffles, I know what happened there. I can see it in my mind clear as day. I don't know what you're smoking, but I really did shoot Joel. And then Poppet shot me, and ... " I swallow back the fear. If I let it, it'll overwhelm and consume me. "Ronnie," I venture, but the woman's already rising from her chair.

"No, Lola. You're confused. A lot happened back there, so it's easy to see why you might not remember the exact sequence of events. Poppet shot you, yes, but you didn't shoot anybody. You were lying on the floor bleeding. Do you understand that?"

My heart is beating like a drum, like one of Ronnie's songs. *What if he's dead?* Nah. Nah. I was awake until ... well, my last few memories there are hazy ones, but I know I remember Ronnie's face looking down at me, his words filling my head and promising that everything was going to be okay. Guess the crazy bloke was right, wasn't he?

"I ... " I think I get what this chick's trying to do. This here's my story and I better stick to it, kind of a thing? "I guess," I hazard a weak affirmative to her intense stare and she curls her lip at me. I lift my hands up in a placating gesture. "Okay, okay, calm ya tits, lady. I didn't shoot anybody. Now can you please tell me what happened to Ronnie McGuire, the drummer for Indecency?"

"I know who Ronnie McGuire is," the woman tells me in a deadpan. *Um, 'kay. That's great. Now how about the whole 'alive' part of the conversation?* I swallow hard and stare into the wide spots of darkness that make up her pupils, pleading, one woman to another. "He's fine." I let out a sigh of relief, and then cringe. Okay. I lied. Even with the morphine, I can still feel the spot where that little fucker pierced through my stomach. "What about my sister? Did she get arrested?" I ask, thinking of the kid clutched in her hand, the crazy gleam in her eyes. That wasn't at all like the Poppet Saints I knew. Wonder what dad would have to say about that one?

The woman turns away like she's not going to answer me and then pauses with her hand on the door, glancing over her shoulder with sympathy. I know before she even says a word that it's going to be bad.

No.

"Your sister's dead."

DOLL FACE

X X X

In the movies, hospitals always shut down at night, and it's real fuckin' easy for the characters to sneak out of their rooms and prowl around. I don't even make it out of *bed*.

"Miss Saints," the nurse exclaims when she comes in to check on me and finds me collapsing to the white linoleum floor. "What on earth are you doing?" she growls as she moves up behind me and hits her hand to a button on the wall. Within fifteen seconds, two more of the bitches appear and drag me back into my bed, upping my medication while I scream slang phrases at them that I'm not even sure *I understand*.

"Go suck pond water, you buggering bushies!" I wail as I let them hook me back up to the machines. I don't even fight. Why bother? A drugged up bitch with a bullet wound is hardly any match for these crazy ladies in their teal colored scrubs, faces hard as stone. I thought nurses were supposed to be *nice*? "You think you're the cat's pajamas? You're nothing but a cattle duffer," I growl at one of them. She gives me a look and a raised eyebrow. Yeah, I know I'm not making any sense, but I just found out my sister's dead, and I'm hyped up on God only knows what. I ain't making any excuses. I spit at one of them and she jerks back, mouth agape. "Put *that* in your juice box and suck all over it." I kick my legs, but the motion only causes me pain, so I quit that pretty quick. "I want to see Ronnie," I tell them, but they're not listening to me anymore, not even when tears begin to fall down my face and soak into the neck of my hospital gown. "My sister's dead," I tell them, but they're already on their way out. "I'll make sure to leave something good in the bedpan for you, you scum dog bitches!"

I sink into the pillows and squeeze my eyes shut, fully prepared to spend a miserable night alone.

"Lola?" My attention snaps to the door and a smiling face belonging to Sydney Charell. She slips inside and moves over to the edge of the bed. I don't know the woman all that well, but I like her, enough that as soon as her fingers curl around mine, I start to sob. "Shh," she whispers, brushing back my hair. I wonder how the hell she got in here. At this point, I'm well aware of the guards that are sitting outside my door. I decide not to even ask. Who cares?

"Ronnie?" I ask her as she tucks my head against her chest and pats my cheek.

DOLL FACE

"He's fine, everyone in Indecency is okay," she ventures, and I know she's thinking about my sister, too. "Naomi's just been moved out of surgery, but she's still in critical condition." I close my eyes and try not to think worst case scenario.

"How many people are dead?" I whisper as Sydney takes a step back. I feel like a smashed crab next to her, snot pouring from my nose, hair tangled, bare foot and dressed in an ass-less hospital gown. Sydney's makeup is perfect, lips rouged in a purple red, tattoos hidden by a long sleeved black sweater and some tight jeans with crazy amazing purple heels.

"Four," she says and then rushes to fill in the blanks. "Stephen, America, Joel, and ... " She doesn't bother to finish her sentence. She doesn't need to. We both know what name goes in that particular blank. *Poppet.* My heart constricts and squeezes a few last tears down my face. I promise myself after that that I won't cry anymore. What's the fucking point? Poppet was dead long before she physically passed away. Hell, the girl I knew shriveled away in France before she ever showed up here. Can't give Stephen/Tyler all the credit. "I came here because I knew they were probably keeping you in the dark." Sydney looks around at the shadowed room. Stupid bitch nurses turned the lights off on me when they left. "Didn't know that was a literal thought."

"Give it to me, babe. All of it. Tell me what special brand of shit's been smeared across the wall of my life. I want to hear it." I sniffle and wipe my arm under my nose. Sydney sighs and looks around for something to sit on. There's an ugly chair in the corner, clean but covered in a fabric that I'd label *baby puke pink.* She drags this over next to the bed and sits down with a sigh, pulling off her heels and tucking her legs up by her side. "I wasn't going to ask, but fuck it, I want to know anyway. How'd you get in here?"

A smile lights Sydney's lips, but not a happy one, a twist of her mouth that says she's resigned to her station in life, even if she really does want something better.

"A wad of green I got from cashing one of my brother's checks plus breast implants and some sweet talking equals free entry. And that's just for the hospital staff. Brayden's people let me in without taking a dollar. Somehow though, I feel like the price I'm going to pay is a hell of a lot higher."

"No hand jobs? Got in pretty easy then. I must not be as important as I thought. Damn it, ego, you lied to me." Sydney laughs, and I smile, but it doesn't last long. Poppet's face flashes in my brain, but not the new Poppet

DOLL FACE

with the crazy eyes and the blonde hair, the old one with a snippy attitude and a head of rich brunette, like yours truly. Her hair was always prettier than mine though, like coffee without cream. Mine's the color of a stale Tim Tam, one that's been left under the sofa for weeks before you find it. Granted, I'd still gobble it up, but then that's just me.

"Well, if that's the case, then I'm shit on the bottom of your shoe. *Nobody* gives a flying fuck about me." Sydney doesn't even sound upset when she says this, tucking some of her blonde hair behind an ear.

"Not even Dax?" I ask, liking the direction this conversation is going. I don't want to talk about the concert or my sister or Stephen or anything else for that matter. Sydney snorts and then sweeps both her hands over her hair, pushing back the pale strands as she sighs.

"I don't know. I mean, we just met. Sure, we had some chemistry, but what the hell does that really mean other than *great sex*." She shrugs like she doesn't give a shit, but I'm an expert when it comes to smellin' crap. "Granted, we only got to do it once … " Sydney taps her nails on the arm of her chair and then forces a smile. Her blue eyes meet mine and we share one of those looks, the kind chicks always get when they're talking about men. It's a look that says *hey, we like your penis but your attitude could use some fuckin' work.* "Anyway, why are we talking about Dax again?"

"Because I really don't want to talk about anything that matters." My chest gets tight, and I imagine my sister, holding one of our lorikeets on her arm. The bird's bright colors clashed with the ugly tie-dye crap she was wearing, her teeth too white against her dry lips as she smiled at me and I threw a tube of lip balm at her face. It's not a memory that means much, has no real significance, no epic music playing in the background, but it's stuck there in my head on a continuous loop. I look away from Sydney and focus on the floor. "So. Sex once. That sucks."

"Yep. Once. In the back of a strip club. He was a little buzzed, I guess." Sydney growls under her breath, drawing my attention back to her with a smile. I like a woman who knows what she wants. I can tell Miss Charell here wants Dax and his ding-a-ling, even if she won't admit it. "And then we found his dead friend and Hayden killed herself, so … " Sydney shrugs. "Let's just say *budding romance* hasn't exactly been in his vocabulary." She looks up at me. "But you. You're in love with Ronnie."

I wet my lips.

DOLL FACE

I haven't admitted it out loud, so I struggle with my response for a moment.

"Yeah."

"Yeah?" Sydney asks and I give her a look and a raised eyebrow.

"What do you want me to say: *yes, of course.* Yeah, yeah, I think I love him." Sydney rolls her eyes to the ceiling and starts rubbing her feet with her hands, giving herself a foot massage. I get it. Wear heels enough and you'll start doing it, too. It's something men never fuckin' understand. No, you can't park down the Goddamn block. No, it's not *just* a short, little walk to me, asshole. You like the way this butt looks in these shoes? Drop me off at the fucking door.

"You mean you know you do." She leans over and I think about the hazy image I have of her, grabbing my gun, holding off ... *somebody* from behind Ronnie and me. Without her, he might've been killed. I don't know what happened, but I owe her a thanks anyway, even if she's starting to piss me off. "I saw you choose him over you."

"I chose to let myself get what I deserved." I point at my stomach. "Which is ten times worse than this. I put on a mask, hopped Naomi's bus and helped beat a girl to death. Is there any making up for that crime? Don't think so." I sigh and lay back into the pillows. I'm happy to be alive because that means I get to see Ronnie again, but I almost think it might've been easier if I had died. No matter what might've happened – heaven, hell, rebirth, the river fucking Styx, or even total blackness – it would've washed the guilt away. I could've started fresh. Even if I ended up shoveling coal in some magma pit in the center of the earth, getting the Devil's horns shoved up my ass day in and day out, at least there'd be the sense of atonement. I could know that the girl I wronged, she was getting her revenge.

"Okay, okay, fine. Your self-sacrifice had absolutely nothing to do with Ronnie McGuire." Sydney sighs and shakes her head. We might not have known each other all that long, but I can see she already gets exactly where it is that I'm coming from. *That bitch.* "So do you want to keep talking about Dax or should I fill you in?" I groan and turn my face away, but I know have to hear this stuff sooner or later. Might as well be sooner. Maybe the drugs the nurses gave me will help disseminate the information through my brain?

"Out with it then," I groan, feeling my lashes flutter. Getting shot makes a bitch tired like nothing else. "Commence the breakdown of the sinister plot, complete

DOLL FACE

with cackling. Can you gleefully rub your hands together while you do it?"

"If it'll make you feel better, I'll try," Sydney says with a small chuckle. The amusement in her voice fades quick as it came though, right about at the moment she starts to tell me the sordid tale.

Here are the plot points as I see 'em: America killed Travis because she was a crazy bitch, Stephen thought the kid was his and raised it until America decided to hit him over the head with the truth, demanded Stephen relinquish said child to her, and then the two of them set into destroying one another in the most maniacal, egotistical, sociopathic ways possible.

That about sum it up? Any fucking questions?

I groan and clamp my hands over my ears. If only Cohen Rose had died along with Joel, then at least there'd be some good news coming out of this. *I hope he gets his tiny penis stuck in a door and it falls the fuck off. It's so little, it'd be almost impossible to find.* The thought's almost enough to make me smile, at least enough to make me drop my hands to my lap.

"So why are you here anyway, at the hospital I mean?" I ask when Sydney finishes and a tense silence settles over the room. I listen as she shifts in the chair and then yawns. I follow up with one of my own. In a minute here, I'll be drifting off to sleep, drowning in a blissful blackness that better damn well not include anymore octopus penis monsters.

"Brayden Ryker spirited away the other bands. I'm not in a band. I got left behind and ended up wrangling a ride to the hospital on Naomi's ambulance. I told them I was her sister." I laugh, but Sydney doesn't echo the sound, coming over to stand next to me with a solemn expression in her blue eyes. "Whatever you say or do around Brayden's people, be careful. I can't tell if they're the good guys or the bad guys. Since I don't really believe in either, I'd say, take them with a grain of salt." I'm instantly reminded of Poppet. *Lola, this isn't about good versus evil. There's no such thing. It's just about us versus them.* "Sleep tight, lady," Sydney says, giving my hand a squeeze before making her way out of the room and closing the door carefully behind her.

The whisper of it snapping into place is the loneliest sound I've ever heard.

CHAPTER 4
※ Ronnie McGuire ※

Three days in a crappy ass motel with dirty water and barely fucking there basic cable. Sounds like many a long weekend I've spent shooting up and passing out, only to wake up and start the process all over again. Here's the thing though, take that equation but subtract the drugs and add Turner Campbell in a melancholy rage and you've got my weekend splattered in shit across a public toilet.

"Man, can you please sit down?" I beg him, glad that the guards are finally gone, leaving us to our own personal hell. I guess they figured, hey, they're ten stories up and there are bars on the windows. The only way out of here is to take turns drowning each other in the dirty ass toilet. Even then, only one of us would be lucky enough to jump ship. "Pacing the raggedy ass carpet isn't going to get you more information." I flip through our limited selection of fuzzy TV channels, looking for some sort of news station. I find a few, but the sound's so fucked up that all I can do is read the blurbs that flash across the screen every now again. The ticker on the bottom still says *the new lead singer for rock band Amatory Riot is still in critical condition at UCLA Medical Center.* After that flickers by, there's some football news, political mumbo jumbo, and a story about a dog who saved his owner from a house fire. Fascinating shit. "I will tell you the *instant* I see anything new to report."

Turner keeps pacing, ignoring me for the third day in a row. We're basically prisoners in here – despite the fact that Mr. Ryker promised we could leave at any time. The asshole hasn't been back since his initial visit and only Milo's allowed to come and go. He drops food off, brought us our bags full of fresh clothes, but that's about it. According to the guards out front, we leave or break their shitty ass rules and it's hashtag game fucking over. Lola shot Joel; Naomi shot America. I don't know how they're going to escape this mess without any jail time,

DOLL FACE

but if hanging out here will give them a shot at it – and it will, according to these assholes – then it's worth the pain.

I sigh.

I haven't been able to figure out what's going on and nobody seems willing to tell me, so I sit here and watch the news and wait for the sound to come back on, reading the miniscule amount of text available to me for information. Our latest fuckup – a concert that's achieved international attention – is on every Goddamn station, so it's not hard to find someone that's talking about it. What's hard to stomach is the misinformation and half-truths that are floating around. Poppet's being played off as a stalker, a girl who joined her sister on the tour and then fell in love with Stephen Hammergren – the CEO of Spin Fast Music Group who was so personally interested in Amatory Riot and Indecency that he decided to show up for the concert at America's invitation. I mean, now that word's gotten out, it's well-known that they used to be lovers who had a child together. The media has spun this tale, turning Poppet into a crazed girl so desperate for Stephen's affections that she was willing to kill for them.

This leaves ... a lot to be desired in my opinion. A lot of people were hurt, several people died, Naomi was *seen* leveling her gun at America and pulling the trigger. None of the media stations talk about this part of the equation. I can't get online, so I have no idea what the social media shit storm looks like, but I can't imagine it's any good.

I groan and let my arm flop over my eyes.

Really makes me miss the early days of driving from gig to gig in our van, begging free overnight stays at the houses of fans, peddling our crappy ass demo to anyone that would listen. Back then, Asuka was with us, so was Travis. I thought I hated it then, but I know now that that was fucking heaven.

"Turner, *please*," I beg because I can't take it anymore. His negative energy is creating this vortex of emotion that's pulling my soul into the center of the room, ripping it straight from my body, limb by limb. I feel sick to my stomach. "I can't watch you do this to yourself. I don't know how long we're going to be stuck in here, so can we please make the best of it?"

"They can't keep us in here, cut off from the fucking world like this," he growls, but he has yet to test the assholes and see if they really will just let us walk out. If it's bothering Turner that much, we can go, but I feel like if we're going to get even an iota of truth out of the situation, we have to stay. If it means sitting here on this mustard yellow bedspread and staring at a TV set from

DOLL FACE

1992, I'll do it. And I'll do it with a fucking smile on my face. For Lola.

I turn the TV off and sit up, watching Turner pause just long enough to glare at me before he gets his shit together and shakes his hands out with a grumbling sigh.

"Do you want to talk about it?" I ask, and he scowls at me.

"No, Ronnie, I don't want to frigging talk about it. I really, really don't, okay? Stop being such a fucking girl and act like a man. Clam up and refuse to show any emotion except anger." I laugh, but Turner doesn't even smile. Guess he wasn't trying to be funny. "Nice that you can find humor in the situation," he snarls, moving towards the edge of the bed and leveling his glare on me. Turner's brown eyes are bloodshot from lack of sleep, and his hands are shaking like he's on a freaking comedown.

"I'm not trying to make fun of you, man. I'm not poking fun at your pain, you know that." I touch a hand to my chest and sit up as Turner slumps down to the edge of the bed and drags his hand down his face.

"Yeah, yeah, I know. I just ... " Turner sighs and drops his hand to his lap, looking over at me with a sad-sack expression I'm more used to seeing in the mirror. *Shit.* "I'm no good at sitting idle. I'm nobody's fucking prisoner."

I push myself to my feet with a groan. I am now officially, one hundred percent clean and sober, and it *sucks*. I would kill for some dope right about now. Shit, I can practically *feel* it in my blood, stirring up the dopamine in my brain, tellin' me that hell yeah, I'm happier than a fucking crocodile in a room full of sheep. But it's not real, and it won't change anything in the long run. Trust me, I know. For ten years I've self-medicated and fucked around and for ten, long ass years, I've been living under a cloud. Lola's like the sunlight that burns away the fog. Turner might call me a douche for saying that, but in his heart, he'd know it was true.

"Do you trust these fuckers?" Turner asks, shoving his sweatpants down his hips and flashing me some white and red plaid boxers and an old bandage wrapped around his thigh. Turner yanks the gauze back and stares at the bullet wound, poking at the shiny pink edges with his fingernail. It looks like it's on its way to being healed, but he still cringes when he touches it.

"Not really, no. But if there's a chance, even just a slim one, that Naomi could get through this without having to stand trial for murder, wouldn't you take it? Brayden obviously has connections and even though I personally think he blows dick at security detail, I believe

DOLL FACE

he has the ability to help clean up this mess. Why he's even bothering with America gone is beyond me, but can we give it two more days?" My friend grunts but keeps his attention focused on the wound in his leg. Maybe, like me, he's comparing that wound to whatever happened to those girls, magnifying the pain in his head, trying to imagine what it'd be like to take one through the torso.

"Fine. Two days, and then I am fucking out of here. Even another forty-eight hours jammed in here with you sounds like hell." Turner scowls at me, swiping a tattooed hand through his hair before standing up and fixing his pants. "Nothing to fucking do in here except jack off and watch sitcom reruns."

"What fresh hell is this?" I ask him with a slight smile as he moves away and tries to look out the window. It's so grimy and the bars on the outside so thick that there's really nothing to see. As far as I know, we might not even be in L.A. anymore. On the ride over here, we were both so out of it that I don't think either of us even remembers leaving the van and tromping into the elevator.

"When we get out of here, I'm buying an ostentatious house in Malibu or Santa Monica or something." Turner pats down his pockets looking for cigarettes and comes up empty. We've been bumming the occasional smoke off the guards, but for whatever reason, they refuse to just go out and buy us a fucking pack. With a sigh, Turner stops searching and leans his forehead against the window. "Something that costs an arm and a leg, with a dozen bedrooms, and a fucking bowling alley. We'll all move in, have one big Indecency crash pad." He turns to look at me and I raise an eyebrow. "Naomi and I will start a family, and we'll get custody of your forty-nine children." When he closes his brown eyes, I can see that the fear is still there, but there's also a glimmer of hope.

We're going to make it through this.

What the other side will bring, I have no fucking idea.

Two days later and Brayden Ryker still hasn't shown up. Turner and I have both finally hit our breaking point and are gearing up to go. I shower, fix my hair and don some eyeliner, snatch some shades and dress in a black Indecency shirt and some jeans – brand new ones that

DOLL FACE

Milo snuck into my bag at some point. First thing we're doing when we walk out of here, hitting the hospital. I have to look good for Lola.

"I see you've hit the end of the line with your patience," Brayden says, slipping in the door and not bothering to close it behind him. In the hallway, I catch a glimpse of Jesse and my lips split into a grin. He gives me a thumbs-up and for the first time in days, I feel like I can breathe. "My apologies. I only expected to keep you here for t'ree days." Turner wrinkles his nose at the man's accent and shakes his head, imitating the word *three* under his breath. Brayden shrugs and then moves aside, like that's it. When neither Turner nor I move, Brayden holds out a hand and gestures for us to go.

"We're done here?" I ask, and he shrugs. "No explanation, no debriefing, just get the hell out and go?"

"On the way to the hospital – where I presume you'd like to go – you'll get your stories straight. You saw what we say you saw and that's it. I did the best I could, to try to make up for the mess you were dragged into, but my reach only goes so far. America and Stephen might be dead, but that doesn't mean things are going to be easy. I'll be in touch." Brayden scoots away and disappears down the hallway before I get out another question. I clench my teeth, but what am I gonna do? Chase the man down? His biceps are as big around as my fucking waist.

Turner and I join Jesse in the hallway, pausing for an awkward moment of bro hugs, wherein I'm encouraged to show most of the affection since, you know, that's been designated as my job. Jesse runs a hand over his short hair with barely a grimace. When he first got it cut, just a single touch was enough to send him into a full blown man-trum. Looks like he's finally over losing his locks.

"Where's Milo?" I ask, hitching my bag up on my shoulder and giving the guards at the end of the hallway a sideways glance. "And Trey?"

"Waiting downstairs," Jesse says with a sniffle, rubbing at the pinup tattoos on his arm. The buxom beauties stretch over his muscles with bright smiles and daring winks, scandalous lingerie and dresses that manage to hark back to an earlier era while simultaneously encouraging dirty thoughts. I never gave the tattoos much thought before, but now that I know Jesse's gay, I have to wonder if they're some sort of front for the world.

"What do you know?" I ask as Turner shoulders past us and moves towards the elevators, scowling at the guards as they step aside and let us on. I ignore them, focusing on Jesse's brown eyes as he looks at me and

DOLL FACE

shrugs.

"Nothing I'm sure you haven't already figured out." There's an awkward pause as the ratty elevators doors screech closed and I'm left wondering if we're even going to make it downstairs. The damn thing feels like a tin can on a string – only that'd be safer. There's a questionable stain on the orange carpet near my foot and the walls are so covered in old movie posters that it's impossible to see if there are actually any walls behind the curling bits of paper. Doesn't bother me much. Again, kind of used to this scene. Indecency spent a good couple of years living in exactly this sort of squalor, so we get it. At the time, it felt appropriate, especially after Asuka and Travis passed away, like I deserved the filth and the echoing screams from the rooms next door. "Was that really Travis' son onstage?"

"That was so fucking him," Turner says, still growling and snapping at everyone in sight. Apparently, being set free hasn't cooled his rage. Nothing will, I don't think, until he gets a chance to see Naomi. "The long arms, the freckles on the back of his neck, the way his lower lip curved up in the center, like an upside down bow tie. Call me a bitch or whatever for getting all poetic, I don't care, but I know my best Goddamn friend's sperm when I see it."

C.M. Stunich

"That's ... disturbing, to say the least," I tell Turner, but I'm only trying to cheer him up again. It's not a role I'm used to, but it feels like a role I was born for. Come to think of it, I guess in bits and pieces, I've been doing this all along. Only, when I was lecturing or encouraging before, it was to keep people from ending up where I was, trying to stay lonely in my pit of misery and hell. Now, it's to elevate them up to where I've climbed. Big fucking difference. "Anyway, you're right. America and Travis really *did* have a child together apparently." I purse my lips, thinking of the poor kid. After what he just went through, he's got to be traumatized beyond belief. And now both his parents are dead. Who gets custody? "I wish we could raise him," I say absently, but I know that's a pipe dream if I've ever heard one. The courts would *never* grant custody of a child to any of us – and that includes me. If either Lydia or Phoebe's families challenge me in court, I will lose the legal custody I now have over them. Of that, I'm sure. I need to make nice with them and soon, before the fact that my name is printed on the birth certificates becomes less than enough for me to keep my daughters.

I grit my teeth.

Ever hear the phrase *full plate*? Well, my plate isn't just full but overflowing. It's like fucking Thanksgiving

DOLL FACE

up in here.

"Would you like a ride to the hospital?" one of the guards asks. I've been desperately trying to tell them apart, but they're all average height, average build, brunette, nothing remarkable to take note of. I'm sure Brayden didn't arrange his team like that by accident.

"Nah," Turner says, holding up his hands and spinning away from the guards. He backs out of the elevator, shaking his head. "I think you've done enough," he whispers roughly, and then he's turning and tearing down the hall towards Milo, holding his hand out and wiggling his fingers. "Cell phone, now."

"Mr. Campbell," Milo says, his voice beyond exhausted. The bags under his eyes now extend all the way down his cheeks, sagging across his face like bruises, and his blonde hair is wild and unkempt, not at all like I'm used to seeing. I think our manager might need a raise. He lifts his blue eyes away from Turner and focuses them on me with a slight ghost of a smile. "Mr. McGuire."

"Cell phone," Turner repeats, his eyes closed, hand trembling. "Give it to me." Milo sighs and basically tosses his phone at Turner, who's so obsessed with getting online and looking for news about Naomi that he doesn't even complain.

"This feels weird," I admit to Milo and he nods, running a hand down his face. His ivory colored tie is stained, and the white shirt underneath it drenched in sweat. His gray suit jacket is crooked and hanging loosely off one shoulder, giving him a lopsided appearance that makes me queasy. "Are you okay?" Our manager takes a deep breath, like he's really doing some soul searching in that split second of time we spend milling in the dirty hallway. I lick my lips and offer up a solution that I know is only fair, but which hurts nonetheless. "If you want to quit and walk away now, you can." Milo snaps his gaze to mine and his pale blue eyes go wide. I keep talking before he gets a chance to protest. "You can have half of whatever I've made on this godforsaken tour. We've put you through too much."

Milo purses his lips.

"I'm content with the contract we put in place at the start of this journey together and I'm determined to see it through." Milo shakes his head and grabs onto the back of Trey's wheelchair. The groupies are gone, the entourage has dissipated, and it's just the five of us alone in a grubby hallway with nowhere to go, just like the olden days.

DOLL FACE

"Milo," I begin, but he's not done, his harsh voice snapping Trey out of his nap.

"I have no family, Ronnie." He glances over his shoulder at me. "I'm forty-five years old, and I have nobody and nothing. This is my life now, and as horrible and stressful as it might be, I enjoy it. You boys give me a purpose above and beyond a job description. If I leave, God only knows what'll happen to you. Stop offering to let me go as a favor. It would simply be a curse." Milo sniffs and starts pushing the wheelchair towards the doors and out into the sunshine. It smells so fucking bad out here that I just *know* we're still in L.A.

I pause on the pavement and stare at the white van sitting in front of the entrance. It's one of three cars in the parking lot. Considering the other two are missing their wheels and have no windows, my guess is that this beautiful baby belongs to Brayden's people.

"Let me guess," I say as I squeeze my fingers tight on my bag and let my gaze wander the mostly empty street. Across from us, there's an abandoned warehouse covered in graffiti. A block to my right, three guys with their pants hanging around their asses and cigarettes clutched between their fingers. They pass plastic baggies of goodies around while I try not to salivate. *I need a hit so bad. So, so bad.* "You are going to give us a courtesy lift to the hospital whether we like it or not?" I turn and glance over my shoulder at Brayden's men. The one on the right shrugs and I sigh.

Oh well.

Even though it feels like it's all over – the tour, the music, the drama – I'm not upset. There are no paparazzi here, no roadies trying to bum smack off me, it's almost … peaceful.

Too bad we all know that shit ain't gonna last.

CHAPTER 5
LOLA SAINTS

Hospitals are weird. I decide after a couple of days that I don't much care for 'em. How can a place be both lonely and crowded at the same time? There are sour faced nurses everywhere and doctors who act like they've got better things to do, scowling at you when they think you're not looking and saying derogatory crap under their breath. Without even trying to get to know me, everyone here's assumed that because I'm involved in what's sure to be considered one of the most infamous tours in human history, that I must be a cunt. Or at the very least, *a slutty little asshole* as Nurse Dina refers to me.

I lay on my back in the hospital bed, one hand thrown

over my eyes as I pray away the sun and wish for rain. It would fit my mood better. Sitting in this sterile little room with no flowers and no company? It might as well be a jail cell. At least if I was in the big house though, I'd probably get better food. And maybe, just maybe, I'd be able to roll over onto my side.

The door opens and I groan, expecting Nurse Dina again. That bitch is *punctual*. But I'm not ready for her yet. Next time she comes 'round, I'm gonna take a nice, long hot piss in the bedpan, so she has something to clean up.

"Can't I have a moment of fucking peace?" I ask, pulling my arm away from my eyes and freezing as I catch sight of the person standing at the foot of my bed.

My heart starts to pound and my head gets real dizzy, like I'm half-cut and already slamming my next drink. I have to swallow three times before I can speak.

"Ronnie?" My head is pounding now, or maybe that's just my heart, echoing around inside my chest and ricocheting up to my skull. I promised I wasn't going to cry again, but the stupid tears start to fall anyway, and I suddenly can't think of anything but my sister and how her dead body must look, all stiff and splattered in blood. How am I supposed to tell my dad that his little girl is

DOLL FACE

gone? Why the fuck didn't she stay in France making Camembert cheese for fuck's sake?

"Don't cry, doll face," he tells me and my heart flips, like a teenager girl getting a smile from the boy she likes. Such a small gesture can make a big difference when your life's as fucked as mine. I purse my lips together and let the tears fall as Ronnie makes his way around the end of the hospital bed and gathers me against his chest. I grunt at the pain in my side, but it doesn't matter. Nothing matters except for this. My fingers curl in Ronnie's T-shirt while the down under bits of me swear up and down that a little gunshot ain't enough to stop this train. I push back a completely inappropriate wash of hormones and bury my head in his chest, taking deep breaths to hold back the sobs. Ronnie tangles his hand in my hair, brushing the stray strands back from my forehead with his inked up fingers, the four purple hearts dancing dangerously across his skin. "I'm sorry about Poppet," he whispers, and I nod, sniffling and trying to put on a brave face.

"Me, too," I reply, leaning back and trying to smile up his face. He's shaved for me, cleaned up real nice. There's a dash of eyeliner around his eyes and the faintest hint of dark circles, but Ronnie looks sober and oh so happy to see me. The gleam in his brown eyes warms as he bends down and presses his lips to my forehead, giving me the chills. The last boyfriend I had was Cohen Rose and he sure as shit didn't give me chaste kisses on my forehead. *I was willing to die for this motherfucker right here, that's a big deal.* I look away and try to wrap my emotions tighter around myself, before Ronnie can pick up on them. He's good at that crap, you know? I slide my eyes back to his, trying to keep my expression neutral. "But she made her choice, and I made mine."

We stare into one another's eyes for a moment before the door opens again and Turner Campbell stumbles in, slumping into the baby puke pink chair in the corner. His face is bare and empty, but not devastated. There's a big difference, like a concert venue that's been evacuated instead of burned down. Get the picture?

"Naomi's still alive," he whispers, his voice quivering like my hands as they sit idle in my lap. I force them to stay still and watch Ronnie's friend sink deeper into himself. "But she's not awake yet. They're not even sure if she *is* going to wake up. And they won't let me see her because I'm not fucking family," Turner growls with a frustrated snarl, leaning over his knees and staring at the while linoleum floor beneath his boots. "Same situation as with Trey. Why don't people understand that fucking *family* isn't relegated to two parents and their kids. I hate

DOLL FACE

this Goddamn shit." He kicks out his leg and hits the little two seater table that's sitting empty in the middle of the room. It screeches across the floor and slams into the wall before coming to a stop.

"It sucks, Turner, I know, but Naomi is going to make it. Then you two can get married, and next time one of you gets shot at a concert, you'll have hospital privileges." Ronnie tries to smile, but Turner's not having any of it, frowning and turning his attention to the empty wall.

Ronnie looks back at me, and I stare into his face, wondering how we ended up here. It was a weird set of circumstances, I'll give you that.

"You look beautiful," he tells me and I snort.

"What do you think this is, bush week?" I ask, and he gives me a weird look. Aw, nobody understands poor Lola Saints and her crazy arse little mouth. I'll admit, I've been known to make up a word or two in my day, but that shit right there is legit. "Never mind," I say and Ronnie chuckles. "Let me translate for you: you're not fooling anyone with that shit. I look like roadkill, and I know it. These bitches won't let me do anything, not even get out of bed. They're making me piss in a bedpan. Yesterday, they tried to give me a sponge bath, but I spit in Nurse

Dina's face. Now she won't even get me a cuppa and I'm jonesing for some caffeine." I take Ronnie's hand in mine and give him a pleading look. "Get me a cup of coffee, will ya? Something that doesn't suck. No doubt you'll have to leave the hospital to get a hold of it. Everything in here is poison, I tell you. *Poison.*" Ronnie pulls me to his chest again and my body shivers. It's a lot easier to joke around than it is to stay serious.

"That I can do," he promises as we hold each other and I wonder frantically how this is all going to play out. Where do we go from here? Are Ronnie and I a couple? I mean, not really. We hardly know each other, right? Even if I think I'm in love with him, that doesn't seal our fate, doesn't bind us together permanently. Do I go back home and tell my dad in person that Poppet is dead? Unless he already knows. I have a feeling that our fuckups might be screwed up enough to cross the Pacific Ocean. Either Ronnie is psychic or he can tell from the stiffness of my shoulders and my sudden silence what I'm thinking. "Stay here with me, Lola," he says, and I swallow hard. "In Los Angeles for a little while. We can rent a house or something, get our heads together, just hang out. I'll take you to Disney Land or some shit." I snort as he slides his fingers across my jaw and makes my lashes flutter.

DOLL FACE

"I hate Mickey Mouse," I admit and Ronnie laughs. "Scares the crap out of me, won't lie about that." *But I like your offer,* I think, knowing that Ronnie feels the same way I do. Question is, how do I get up the courage to really talk about? "Can we rent a house on the beach? I think we deserve a little sand and surf after all that fucking shit."

"Nobody's renting anything," Turner grumbles and we both glance over at him, sitting slumped and lonely in the hospital chair. "I'm buying an Indecency crash pad, somethin' real, real nice."

"Turner," Ronnie says, but his friend isn't listening. He's sliding his finger across the screen of a smartphone, brow furrowed and lips turned down at the corners.

"A dozen bedrooms, some fancy ass kitchen stocked with energy drinks, and a pool I can spend most of the day naked in." He's still mumbling, but his lips are twitching. That's a good sign, right? Ronnie sighs and looks back over at me with a shrug. "We might not be able to go back on tour anytime soon, but that doesn't mean life as we know it has to be over." Turner doesn't exactly sound like he believes that, but I decide not to say anything. If I can get out of this hospital sooner rather than later, I'd live in an alley behind a fast food restaurant. A big house with Ronnie sounds like a dream, even if all his friends are living in it, too.

"Whatever you want, man," Ronnie says with another shrug as he leans down and puts his chin on my head, holding onto me like we're a proper couple and all that. Sure, we've been spending a lot of time together, but ever since I found out Poppet was willingly with Stephen, I've been in a funk. Drunk, fucked up, or sleeping. That's how I've spent most of the last week. Getting shot and waking up to find myself still breathing? Now if that doesn't give me a kick in the arse, I don't know what will. I think of Poppet again and my throat closes up.

Before I can think up anything else to say, that uppity bitch, Nurse Dina, waltzes into the room and piddles around like she's got something important to do. I notice she says longer than her usual five minutes, eyes shifting to the side like a fucking croc searching for prey. I can just imagine this woman with water up to her eyeballs, scanning along the shore for an unsuspecting man to waltz on by. If I had to guess, I'd say her cunt's drier than the Great Victoria Desert.

"Why don't you go do what you gotta do and then piss off?" I ask her when her attention gets a little too focused on Ronnie's chest. I'll admit, the man's cleaned up good in the last few weeks. When we first started the tour, he was a grubby little thing with bloodshot eyes and shaking hands. Sure, he still had a handsome face but it was hidden under all that sour. Now, he's dressed up nice, smells clean, expression clear. I can't take all or even any of the credit for that, but I would like to take a piss on him and let the world know that at least for now, he's mine.

"I don't tolerate rudeness," Nurse Dina sniffs, running her hands down the front of her scrubs. She's such a tightwad bitch, I think she'd look more at place in one of those old fashioned nurse's outfits, the pink ones with the short skirts they used to wear way back when. The woman can't be a day over thirty, but she acts like my dead grandma – only twice as stiff.

"How's this for rudeness?" I ask when she jerks an IV needle from my arm with more force than I feel is necessary. "Why don't you pull your lip over your head and swallow? Then, when you take a shit you can get a real good look at how the world sees you?" Dina has no reaction, but Ronnie laughs, stroking my hair back while the nurse fiddles around and does whatever it is that she needs to do.

"Is there a doctor I can speak to about getting her discharged?" he asks, and Nurse Dina actually smiles for the first time since I've been here.

"Nothing would please me more, Mr. McGuire," she says, and I frown. The fact that she knows Ronnie's last name is just more proof that she's desperate for some Indecency dick. I cross my arms over my chest as Ronnie gives me another kiss on the top of my head and moves away with a promise to return.

A moment later, Turner scoots over and stands next to me, flashing a multi-fucking-million dollar house in Beverly Hills on the smartphone's screen. When I glance up at him, there's a wicked gleam in his eye and a dangerous curl to his lip.

"That's bloody outrageous," I choke, shaking my head. I have no idea how much money Indecency's made, but a house that costs more than the national wealth of a small country? Hah. "That's a pipe dream if I've ever heard one."

"This is the house I'm going to buy," Turner growls, pressing the phone against his chest and taking a deep breath. "From trailer park trash to fucking royalty. I'm making this happen." He moves away and heads to the door, pushing it open and grumbling under his breath. I wish him the best of luck, but I know that's never going to happen. Not in a million years.

DOLL FACE

✗ ✗ ✗

"Are you sure you're alright?" Ronnie asks for the third time since I was loaded into this wheelchair. My stomach's still killing me, but the doctors have assured me that if I take it easy, I'll live. They tried to give me some medical mumbo jumbo, but I wasn't listening. I don't care what the bullet hit or didn't hit, only that it passed all the way through me and that I'm lucky as fuck to be alive. That's it.

"Sure as shit, babe," I tell him, smiling when he chuckles and shakes his head like I'm crazy. "Feeling pretty fucking perky right about now. Out of this hospital, away from that bitch nurse … " I trail off as we exit the elevator and head to the lobby, meeting up with Ronnie's manager and his friend, Jesse Decker. It's decidedly peaceful in here right now, just a light trickle of traffic, a few heads turning our way, but no massive crowds, no paparazzi. Pretty incredible if I do say so myself. I start to wonder if the Indecency/Amatory Riot bubble has finally popped. Maybe this time, the drama went too far, and the world's had enough? Hah. I shake my head and touch my fingers to my forehead. I know better than that. This world is bloodthirsty, full of crazy ass people desperate for drama. It's just a matter of time until they find us and sink their teeth in.

"What's our next step here, Milo?" Ronnie asks, pushing my wheelchair up next to the seating area and plopping onto a small sofa. "To be honest with you, I feel kind of ... lost." Milo nods his head and gestures for Jesse to take a seat in one of the cushy chairs. *Swanky little hospital, ain't it? I wonder how much this stay is going to set me back?*

Milo unbuttons his suit jacket and takes a spot opposite Jesse. These boys are lucky to have a guy like that in their corner, somebody that's got his shit together, someone to guide them through the tough times. I'm almost jealous. I sigh and let my eyes close for a moment, thinking of Ice and Glass and our final performance. It was pretty good – I'll give you that – but our band is as good as dead now. Joel is ... I *killed* him. My second murder this year and I'm not sitting behind bars. I'm not sure how I should feel about that. I swallow hard and open my eyes back up to look at Milo.

"Obviously, the tour is over. It should've ended a long time ago," he whispers, looking away, like this whole thing was his fault. But I know it wasn't. It was mine. And Stephen's. And America's. Milo clears his throat.

DOLL FACE

"But that doesn't mean *Indecency* is over." Milo takes a deep breath and runs a hand over his perfectly styled hair, straight and clean, combed back over his head and gelled into place. He looks a lot more put together than he did this morning, like he somehow found time to shower and change. Good for him. *You go, guy. Kick some ass.* "I sent Josh home for awhile," he says and I glance over at Ronnie, watching his face twitch. Some of us don't have any *home* to go back to. At least Milo seems to be aware of that. "Let's stay in Los Angeles for now, regroup and figure out where to go from here. We need to do a press conference at some point, address all the questions and the rumors. After that, I think it might be beneficial for us to lay low. Perhaps record a new album?"

"I can't think of anything better." We all look up to find Turner Campbell standing over us in his girly lady pants, a mask of self-confidence stamped across his face. I can see right through it, to the pain underneath, but I decide it's best to let sleeping dogs lie. Who am I to call him out on it when I've got enough issues of my own crammed down deep? No judgment here. "I called a realtor and we've got a showing to see the house." He holds up the phone and wiggles it around enticingly, running his tongue across his lower lip and the pair of silver piercings.

"Mr. Campbell," Milo says as he rises to his feet and holds out a hand for the phone. "I understand you've not nowhere to go, but why not start at a hotel? Take some time to recuperate?"

"Because Naomi can't come home to a hotel room." He lifts his chin and crosses his arms over his chest. "The doctors said if she were to stabilize, and I had the right staff to take care of her, that I could take her home."

"Turner," Milo says, in a much softer voice this time. "That would be a decision for her next of kin to make." Turner levels a glare on his manager and lowers his voice to a growl.

"She doesn't have *any* next of kin, Milo. But," Turner pauses and glances around the room, leaning in close, "she *did* appoint a … uh … " Turner looks up at the ceiling like he's trying to think and then snaps his fingers together. "A durable power of attorney for health care." He leans back and tucks his fingers in the back pockets of his pants. Or at least he tries, the Goddamn things are so tight, I'm not quite sure how he manages. "And that happens to be me. *I'm* her power of attorney." Turner sniffs and lifts his chin up like he's inviting argument. No, like he's *desperate* for it. Anything to take the mind off the pain, huh? "Not to mention her fiancé."

DOLL FACE

"Is this something Naomi's going to remember agreeing to when she wakes up?" Ronnie asks, in a very careful tone of voice. Instead of getting angry though, Turner's face shatters like it's made of glass. His brown eyes glaze over and he groans, squatting on the floor and putting his hands over his face.

"She said if she survived the concert, she'd think about it," he whispers. "If she survived." Turner lets out a harsh bark of laughter. "*If.* I should've spirited her ass away, took off and moved to the Bahamas or something." With a grunt, Turner drops to his ass on the linoleum and lifts his face up, letting his hands fall into his lap. "As far as the attorney thing … " He trails off and then sighs again. "Brayden's people set that up, I think. I know sure as shit Naomi never had the time to do something like that. To be honest, I don't even really know what it means, but the doctor said I should've spoken up sooner and that now that I've faxed legal documentation in, I can finally see her. So I did. And I made decisions." His voice cracks and he has to swallow three times before he can speak again. "I want to buy a house, so that I can have Naomi moved there as soon as possible. They've done all they can do with surgery, and now we're playing a waiting game to see if she'll wake up." Turner shrugs his shoulders like he doesn't care, even though it's pretty fuckin' obvious that he does. How many flying fucks does Turner Campbell give about Naomi Knox? Give you a hint ... it's probably somewhere in the range of infinity times infinity.

"Trey woke up, Turner. You believed he would, and he did," Ronnie says, standing up and moving over to his friend. "And when Naomi went missing and everyone else thought she was dead, you believed she wasn't. You've gotta stay in that head space, man, or the worry will kill you." Ronnie's friend glances up at him and nods, pushing himself up to his feet with tight lips.

"I know. I'm just so fucking tired." Turner runs his hands over his face again and takes a deep breath. "Anyway, that's why I wanted to look at this house. I'm planning for the future." Ronnie takes the phone from his friend and raises his eyebrows as he stares at the screen.

"This is a big ass house, Turner. I thought you said we were all moving into suburbia together. Remember the speech? *No beige, no picket fences, and no fucking golden retrievers.* This is a *really* expensive place. I mean, this is a *mansion,* Turner."

"Yeah. It's a mansion that also happens to qualify as a *house* which means I only need to put twenty percent down and pass a fucking credit check. Milo, how much

DOLL FACE

money have we made in the last few months?" Their manager coughs and squirms a little, mumbling something like *it's complicated* under his breath. "Exactly. The answer to that shit is *a lot,* Ronnie. More than we ever could've dreamed of back in the day." Turner grabs the phone back and spins it in a circle. "That's not about to end anytime soon. Do you know how popular we are *now*?"

"As opposed to what?" Ronnie asks, but he looks a little pale.

"As opposed to two days ago." Turner moves past Ronnie and starts off towards the entrance, pausing near the front doors as if to say *what the fuck are you waiting for.* Ronnie looks down at me, and I shrug. He takes the wheelchair and points it towards Turner, dragging Milo and Jesse along behind us.

Everything looks okay through the glass doors. I see sun drenched pavement and a small garden area with four rounded hedges and a smattering of flowers. No crowds. We follow Turner out the front and pause at the edge of the sidewalk while he slips his fingers back in his pockets and chuckles under his breath.

Holy shit.

There are police *everywhere* doing crowd control,

keeping back a mass of people and signs, candles and flowers, away from the entrance of the hospital. They stretch out to either side of us and down the block. Across several lanes of traffic, peering at us through the glittering mechanical river of vehicles that flows in an unending stream, there's even more of them.

"You have got to be motherfucking shitting on me," Ronnie whispers as the gentle murmur of voices comes to a screeching halt. It's like the crowd's a collective whole, a single entity – just like it is during a concert – and those beady little eyes have just landed on us.

Within five seconds, the peaceful mass of people turns into a shouting, screaming wave of human desperation and driving hunger. Their voices rise up and consume us, spearing straight through my skull and out the other side.

"This," Turner says, the sound of his voice hardly audible over the screeching hordes, like an army of demons with twisted souls and gaping maws, white-white teeth, and a path to hell paved with good intentions. "This is what immortality looks like."

CHAPTER 6
⚘ RONNIE MCGUIRE ⚘

Turner Campbell, God bless your heart, I think as the real estate agent grins at us with huge, white teeth. She's wearing a suit that costs more than the rental car we just drove here in, and sweat is pouring down the sides of her face like water. I'm going to take a wild guess here and say it's not just the weather that's got her panties in a bunch.

"I am a *huge* fan," she whispers, voice cracking a bit as Turner lifts his shades and frowns at the multi-million dollar piece of property in front of us like it's not at all impressive. *I can't even believe I'm standing here.* I run my tongue over my lip and try to pay attention to the real estate agent and her two assistants. I think her name's Camby or something like that, but I didn't catch the names of the men behind her. "And let me just say, that I am so sorry for what happened to Naomi." Turner cringes, but he manages to keep that acidic tongue of his in check.

Almost.

"Yeah, well, better help us buy a house and quick. I'm not leaving her at that hospital a day longer than necessary." Turner starts off towards the front doors, forcing Camby to scramble after him. I start to push Lola's wheelchair after them, but she waves her hand dismissively.

"Go," she says, tilting her head back to look up at me. Her beautiful blue eyes put the California Coast to shame. "The view is to fucking die for, and I'd rather you kept Turner from making a complete ass out of himself than spent your time wheeling my handicapped ass around."

"Thank you, babe," I whisper, leaning down to press a kiss to her head. I spare a quick glance for our new security guards. Milo says that this time, *he's* the one that picked them out, but in this private slice of luxury, I'm sure Lola's safe whether these guys are good or not. We had to drive through *two* private gates to get in here and

DOLL FACE

the entire property is surrounded by a stone fence and lush foliage that hides the house from the world. Welcome to Beverly Hills, bitches.

"If I want to move in, like, tomorrow, can that happen?" Turner asks as the real estate agent's assistant holds open one of the two massive front doors for him. He saunters in like he already owns the place, sniffing in approval as his eyes take in the chandelier hanging over our heads. I'm much more cautious, watching as Jesse stumbles in behind Turner and whistles under his breath.

"Oh my God, dude! This is like a castle or some shit," he whispers as Turner's lips twitch into a smile and he glances over his shoulder. The two of them share a fist pump, and I drop my head into my hand with a sigh that Milo mimics.

"From the park to the palace, my friend," Turner growls as the two of them traipse right across the *mosaic marble flooring from Italy* in their combat boots and Converse. The real estate agent scrambles after as I pause next to a grand piano and take a deep breath. Actually, my parents own a house just a few miles away in Benedict Canyon, a one and a half million dollar piece of property that would cost half that in most other parts of the country.

I trail after my friends, through a formal living room with enough custom woodwork to fund a small country's economy for a year. The more I see, the more skeptical I get. I mean, come on. *This place is going to set us back tens of millions of dollars?* Does that number even *mean* anything to Turner? I can barely wrap my head around it.

"Can we really afford this?" I ask Milo Terrabotti as he struggles to keep up with my bandmates, adjusting his tie as he goes. He gives me a very stern look, the skin around his face tight, but better than it was earlier in the day. Sometime between now and then, he found time to shower and change clothes. "Hey, I haven't even *looked* at my bank account since we hired you. I have no clue what kind of wealth we're talking about here."

"Mr. McGuire," Milo says as we emerge into a central courtyard and come face to face with the first of three advertised swimming pools. "Never underestimate the marketability of pain and agony." Milo clears his throat and gives me another look. "Let's just say, if you boys decide not to work another day in your life, you and your families should be well taken care of."

We finally catch up to my friends, standing at the edge of the pool, eyes fixated on the tropical greenery lining the edges, the miniature waterfalls, the artfully placed boulders.

DOLL FACE

"The whole place brings to mind a resort on the Italian Riviera, doesn't it?" Camby says, doing the schmoozing realtor act very, very well. Turner snorts and then spits into the pool which makes Camby turn a funny shade of pink.

"Never been," Turner says, keeping his gaze focused on the perfect blue of the water like he's mesmerized. I look up, at all the palm trees and the broad leaf plants. To our left, there's a string of fancy pool chairs leading to a fire pit. On the wall above it, a TV hangs over the entrance to an outdoor cooking area, complete with refrigerator. Jesus, it'd be nice to live here. I mean, who *wouldn't* want to chill in a mansion in Beverly Hills, but the whole thing just seems ... absurd.

"Turner," I say and he turns slowly to look at me, dropping his shades back into place. The smile stretching across his lips says that, whether I think it's a good idea or not, this is where we're shacking up. All of us. Living together. Might sound a little weird when you think about – four adult men about to hit thirty, moving in with their various girlfriends (if Naomi agrees to this when she wakes up, of course), but for us, this is normal. Since we turned eighteen, we've been traveling together and sleeping in shitty hotels, in the back of our old van. When our music started to take off, we switched to fancy buses and five star resorts, but it's always been the same. Always been us.

I sigh and Turner chuckles under his breath.

"Would you like to continue the tour of the property?" Camby asks, looking at Turner like he's a God that she just doesn't understand.

"Nah, I'm good there, cupcake." Camby nods like she expected this and clears her throat. Turner looks over at Jesse who smiles back at him. If only Trey were here to see. Milo dumped him in a hotel after he dropped us off at the hospital. But Trey does whatever Turner says, just like Jesse. If he was here, the outcome would be the same.

Crap.

Guess Indecency just bought itself a fucking mansion.

My heart starts to race, and my throat gets dry. Turner and Jesse look over at me and we share a mutual look of pain.

"If Travis was here, you know what he'd say, right?" Turner asks as he takes off his glasses again and moves a step backwards, towards the pool.

"That you were a crazy dumb shit, and this is the stupidest idea you've ever come up with?" I suggest as I watch my friend grin and wink at the real estate agent. She's under the impression we're not interested, but she's dead wrong. If she really knew Turner Campbell, she'd know he does absolutely nothing in half-measures.

"He'd say, raise your glass bitches, and let's do this shit." Turner takes another step back, raising his arms out to either side of himself. "Candy," he says, mispronouncing the woman's name. She snaps to like a soldier. "We'll fucking take it."

And then Turner leans back and falls into the pool with a splash that makes Milo cringe and puts a weary smile on my face. *I'm so going to regret this.* I pull a cigarette out of my pants as Jesse whoops and jumps into the pool with our idiot of a lead singer. Camby looks confused but pleased and only one of her assistants wrinkles his nose when I light up my cigarette and watch over the boys like I've always done, like I'll continue to do. Hopefully, now that Lola's here and I'm finally starting to climb out of the hole I dug for myself, I can do a better job.

We'll survive. We'll get through this. Everything is going to be o-fucking-kay.

I close my eyes and take a drag on my cigarette, wishing Travis was here to see this, wishing he wasn't embroiled in a bitter battle that should never have even happened. My friend should be here alive to see his kid, to raise him, to jump in a swimming pool in Beverly Hills. But he's not, and somehow, someway, I'm going to have to find a way to make that right.

XXX

Turner smacks his gum outside the real estate agent's office and surveys the people around us. They're all pretending not to stare, but I can feel their eyes, like lasers. Each look leaves a tiny hole in my skin, a burn that I desperately want to reach my fingers up and itch. I know it's all metaphorical, but I can't help it. We look so out of place in this ritzy ass office, yet nobody blinks an eye at our ratty clothes or Jesse's paint splattered jeans. We're *famous* now and that trumps everything but *rich*. But oh, apparently, we're that, too. I just looked at my bank account. I almost puked at the number, but that was *before* Milo told me that only covers a certain portion of royalties and record sales, that the real money's in touring, merch, and public appearances, that we haven't

DOLL FACE

even gotten paid for a lot of it yet.

"I don't see why we can't just move in tomorrow," Turner's repeating for the fifteenth time since we got here. "I mean, for that much money, somebody should be in here on their knees sucking my dick." I give him a look and he shrugs, worry for Naomi pinching his brow. False bravado aside, I see right through him.

"Real estate transactions take time, Turner," I tell him and he sighs dramatically, sagging into a chair and putting his booted feet up onto someone's desk. I give them an apologetic smile, but the girl sitting behind said desk is staring at Turner with glitter dancing behind her green eyes. I'm sure she doesn't mind. "Just be happy I'm going along with this whole thing. I would've been okay in an apartment building worth a fraction of this place."

"Nah," Turner says, waving his hand dismissively. "You deserve this, Ronnie," he tells me firmly and then pulls his sunglasses off to glare at me. "*Lola* deserves this, don't you think?" I sigh and glance over my shoulder, at Miss Lola Saints as she wheels her chair alongside a row of paintings that hang on the wall like an art gallery. When she sees me looking, she stops moving and smiles back at me. My heart skips a beat, and I have to look away to find the right words.

"I know you worked hard for this," I tell him, because I do. If anyone deserves an extravagant mansion in the hills, it's my friend here. I smile and he rolls his eyes at me because he knows I'm about to get deep. Call it like a sixth sense or something – all my band members have it. "You always told your mom you were going to bury her in the shadow of your Beverly Hills mansion," I say, and although it sounds like a morbid joke to some, we find it funny. You have to laugh about this stuff or the pain will eat you alive inside. Turner started third grade with no teeth, just a bloody mouth and a bunch of excuses. He used to have to sleep in the bathroom of their trailer because it was the only room with a working lock, just to keep a certain kind of step-daddy away. I remember the kids at school picking on him because he smelt bad and his clothes were dirty. I also remember beating the shit out of those same kids.

"Fuck that bitch. She's not good enough to be buried in my backyard." Turner pulls his boots off the woman's desk and flips off the carpet. "Wherever you are, Mom, I hope the flames of hell burn bright." He kisses the tip of his finger with a flourish. A split second later, the real estate agent emerges from her corner office and smiles brightly at us.

"I've got some great news, Mr. Campbell." My friend

DOLL FACE

rises to his feet and we turn to face the woman's blindingly bright smile together. Milo's excused himself to the hall to make some phone calls and Jesse disappeared to the bathroom. I guess it's just me and Turner right now. "We've added in immediate occupancy to your offer and we've also asked the seller to consider allowing you to move in before closing. The property is vacant and does come fully furnished, so that's not a problem. It's just an issue of seeing if the seller will allow you to take temporary residence in the property as a renter." Camby clears her throat and keeps smiling. "It's not normally a situation that a seller's agent would recommend, especially with a property like this, but," Camby bites her bottom lip and takes a deep breath, "both the seller and their agent are huge fans. I asked her to present the offer and I may have hinted that perhaps they could be there when you get the keys?" Turner and I both shrug and Camby nods. "Alright then, we just have a few more details to sort out, and there's a very good chance you could be resting your head in Beverly Hills by tomorrow night."

I take a deep breath and shake my hands out. This isn't just a big deal. This is *huge.* And it's not just the house. There's a part of me that knows as soon as we're settled in here, other, more pressing issues are going to float to the surface. Least of all finding out *exactly* what happened at that concert. The way my mind is programmed, I won't be able to rest until I've got every detail, uncovered every dirty secret, connected every dot. Once I've got a story laid out, I'll feel a hell of a lot better.

And then there's my kids. I think about them every fucking day now – a big change from the random thoughts that used to drift through my brain. I need to get Lydia back from my parents and see about getting Phoebe back from Shannon's. They're not gonna fucking like that. Their daughter was knocked up and abandoned by yours truly and now she's dead. A shiver travels down my spine and I have to tune out what Camby's saying to process the emotions. That's just the tip of the iceberg, too. How someone like me, somebody that's been fucked out of their mind for nearly a decade, is going to handle suddenly having to be a parent to a three year old and an infant is anybody's guess.

I lick my suddenly dry lips and glance back at Lola. If we're going to be a couple, a real couple, and that's all I fucking want in this world, then she'll have to be a part of my daughters' lives. I start wringing my hands, and I can feel a small pool of sweat gathering on my lower back. *Shit. One day at a time,* I tell myself as I try to drag my attention back to the current conversation. *One day at a*

DOLL FACE

time.

Turner shakes hands with Camby, and I follow suit, smiling and nodding at whatever it is she's trying to say. When he turns to walk away, Turner puts a hand on my shoulder.

"Dude, you're getting the ghost look again. What's up?" I look back at my friend and try to take some solace in his strength. The girl I love is here with me, right now, while his soul mate lies comatose in a bed. If he can smile and swagger around and act like an idiot, I can at least pull my shit together.

"Too much thought and not enough action," I say with a sigh. My lips tingle for a cigarette and my skin crawls with the desperate longing for a needle. But I can't do it. No more relapses. If I play my cards right here, I could very well end up with a normal life.

"Jesus Christ, Jesse, you must've been a birthing a Goddamn baby in there. No wonder the bus bathroom was never free."

"Hey, screw you, Turner!" Jesse shouts back, and I sigh, meeting Lola's blue eyes as I feel my lips twitch in embarrassment and barely concealed affection for these assholes. Okay, so maybe a *normal* life isn't on the books for me, but it doesn't mean it can't be a good one.

CHAPTER 7
❈ LOLA SAINTS ❈

Later that night, we're shacked up in a ritzy hotel and I'm finally able to stand up. I wobble like a fucking drunken emu, but I manage. Ronnie's right by my side, his fingers on my hips, his hot breath on the back of my neck. It's the first time we've been alone since the concert on Friday. Fuck, how many days ago was that? It feels like it was both yesterday and an eternity ago. How the hell does that even work?

"Hey, love," I say and feel a slight flush of heat through my body at the word. *Love.* I love Ronnie. I can admit that now. Near death experiences are good for shocking the system like that. Now I just have to figure out how and when I'm going to tell the guy that. "What day of the week is it?"

"It's Friday," Ronnie says and the word feels like it's fluttering against the back of my neck. My fingers curl around the door frame of the bathroom as I try to keep my feet. Collapsing to the burgundy and gold hotel carpet wouldn't exactly be the best way to convince Ronnie I'm feeling good enough for a wrestling match in the sack. "Feels impossible, right? That it's been a week since the concert?"

"Yes and no," I say as he trails his fingers over my side and I turn, putting my back to the wall and looking into his brown eyes. I know there's nothing special about the color, not really, but something about Ronnie's gaze is mesmerizing to me. The depths of his emotions, the intensity with which he feels them, those are rare traits in a man. Hell, those are rare traits in *anybody.* I swallow and drag my eyes away, focusing on the dark window panes to my right.

When Ronnie reaches over and starts to pull up the loose jersey dress I'm wearing, I don't stop him. The lady parts flood like a Goddamn monsoon's brewing overhead, but I know this isn't about sex. He just wants – no, *needs* – to see what happened to me. I close my eyes and let Ronnie have a peek at my first ever official gunshot wound.

"I'm a certified badass now, aren't I?" I joke, but Ronnie doesn't laugh. His fingers travel across the bandages and then pause. I hear his breath hitch as he slowly peels away the gauze. Still, I don't look at him. I can't. Not yet. I wait until I feel the brush of air against the wound before I crack my lids and glance down. "I guess I got lucky," I tell Ronnie, trying to smile. The expression won't stick to my lips. "The bullet passed through, missed my intestines and all that other good stuff in there. Lucky me, right?"

Ronnie takes the dirty bandage and dumps it in the rubbish bin next to the desk before retrieving the bag of supplies the hospital sent us home with. There are some painkillers – nothing I couldn't get from any roadie on the tour though – antiseptic ointment, clean gauze, some medical tape. We're supposed to change the wrappings twice a day. Well, *I'm* supposed to do it twice a day, but I'm lucky – I have Ronnie. I swallow hard, and I know without him even having to say it that he loves me as much, if not more, than I love him. I don't know how or why, but I'm pretty positive he fell for me that first day, when I approached him backstage and pretended to be interested in his assorted collection of gossip and travel stories. That's a drummer for ya. Always intense, focused, always in rhythm. I try not to smile.

His hands are gentle as he cleans the wound and replaces the bandage. I have to look away, not because blood makes me squeamish, but because the soft touch of his hands is too much. Blood and gore, I can deal with. Somebody like this, treating me like I really mean something, I don't know how to process that. My chest heaves and I have a hard time finding my next breath. When Ronnie reaches up and cups the side of my face, I feel tears threatening to squeeze out from under my eyelids.

"I'm sorry about Poppet," he tells me, and his voice is so sincere that I feel sick to my stomach. I can't hold back the wave of emotion when he's looking at me like that, his dark hair falling across his brow, his full lips slightly parted. I lean into his touch and close my eyes again, letting the liquid drip down my cheeks. "I am so sorry that you got dragged into this."

"It's not your fault," I whisper back to him because it's really not, not at all. I should've been stronger, should've told Stephen/Tyler to go fuck himself when he approached Ice and Glass and tricked us into becoming his little minions. I wanted so much to be more than just a sugar farmer's daughter, something more than a girl who'd bet everything on traveling to another country to be with a boy. In all the ways Cohen Rose was rough, Ronnie is gentle. In all the ways he was weak, this man is strong. Maybe, somehow, fate knew I'd end up with Ronnie eventually? If I think about it now, all the pain and the heartache and the guilt, it feels like it was worth it, just to feel the touch of his skin against mine. "I wish I'd been a stronger person."

"You *are* a strong person, Lola Saints. Listen to me." Ronnie's voice brooks no argument, so I glance up and focus on the snake tattoos that wrap his neck. I meet the eyes of a cobra and swallow back another wave of tears. *Fuck.* I keep promising myself that I won't cry, and then I go and do it again. *Damn you, Ronnie.* "If you hadn't fallen prey to Stephen's promises, somebody else would've. Somebody with no conscience, no heart. You came to us and told us the truth, Lola. If you hadn't done that, who knows where this all would've ended up? Believe it or not, things could've been worse."

"Is it over?" I ask, and Ronnie's silence tells me all I need to know.

"*Over* is a relative term," he says, dropping his hand from my face and taking a step back. The soft black cotton of the jersey dress drapes over my form with a swish of fabric and I cross my arms over my chest before looking up at his face. "Here." Ronnie holds out a hand

and smiles at me. I reach out and curl my fingers around his, around the knuckles that spell out *LOVE* in black ink. "Sit down and I'll order room service. You should try to take it easy."

"I've never had it easy," I say and then cringe, realizing how bitchy that sounds. "What I mean is, I'm not sure if I even know how." I move over to the edge of the bed with Ronnie's help and straighten myself out on top of the white linen with a groan. I'm feeling better, and the pain has definitely lessened, but bloody fuck, am I knackered. I close my eyes and rest my head against the pillows, enjoying the gentle reprieve from the chaos that has been my life for the past few weeks. It feels good, too good maybe, because before I know it, I'm asleep.

I must not stay that way for long though because when I wake up, there's a cart next to the bed with silver trays that are still warm when I reach out and touch them. Ronnie's disappeared, but the TV's on, some stupid reality show playing. I sit up and wrap my arms around my chest, staring at the flickering colors with blurry eyes and a yawn. There's a bloke on there wearing high heels and traipsing down a runway. *Perfect.* This is exactly the sort of mindless shit that I love. Nothing dulls the mind better than a healthy dose of 'reality' TV.

I scoot towards the edge of the bed and moan when I swing my feet onto the floor. Getting shot blows some seriously fat donkey dick. Not gonna lie about that one. I touch a hand to my dress and force back the memory of Poppet's face staring back at me. She didn't have to shoot me. She could've dropped that kid's shirt and backed away, held up her hands and said she was sorry. We could've moved on together. I close my eyes against the thought that someday very soon, I'm going to have to call my father. He might already know. Hell, he *must* because nobody's contacted me about funeral preparations.

I open my eyes at the sound of the bathroom door and look up to find Ronnie, freshly showered and *shirtless*. A thrill goes through my body at the lean muscles in his chest and stomach, the thickness of his shoulders and biceps. I can even see a hint of that lily tattoo of his sticking up above the waistband of his black sweats. Brightly colored ink trails down his neck, the snakes' tails wrapping around roses that spill down his side in crimson color. I feel a serious lady boner coming on.

"Well hello, Ronnie," I say and he snorts, moving across the room with the soft whisper of bare feet. He pauses on the other side of the cart and smiles down at me, wet hair hanging in his face. With a brush of his

DOLL FACE

wrist, he pushes it all back and shows me those eyes I love so much.

"I love your accent," he tells me and it's my turn to laugh.

"No, I love *your* accent," I say as I both thank and curse the heavens for this damn cart. If it wasn't here, I'd be dragging him down on top of me, crushing our mouths together, reaching into his pants to find his cock. But then I'd probably be getting a real nasty reminder that I got myself shot last week. I settle for licking my lips and shaking my head in disgust. "You're not allowed to look that fucking hot when I'm this Goddamn injured." I watch as Ronnie removes one of the lids and reveals a hamburger and some hot chips – sorry, *French fries*. "Holy fuck, that looks brilliant. Gimme a damn bite before I pee myself." With another laugh, Ronnie lifts the plate up with one hand and pushes the cart to the side with the other, helping me climb back into bed and setting the food on my lap. He gives me another one of those confusing forehead kisses, the ones that feel too gentle to be real, and I find my heart catching in my throat.

"Did I miss anything?" I ask and Ronnie shakes his head, grabbing his own plate and coming to sit next to me. I watch as he slathers his entire plate in ketchup, and

C.M. STUNICH

I wrinkle my nose. I don't touch the stuff. But I like this, this simple act that tells me something banal about Ronnie. I want to know every boring detail about him – what types of books he likes to read, if he enjoys crappy reality television as much as I do, if he's ever had a real meat pie. He catches me staring as he puts the cap back on the bottle and smiles.

"Turner got a noise complaint filed on him about an hour ago. He had to call and tell me all about it. Also, while you were asleep, Milo dropped off some new phones and some of our personal items. That's about it." Ronnie shrugs as I take a bite of my burger and cringe at the sweetness of the bun.

"Jesus Christ, that shit tastes like fairy floss." Ronnie nearly spits his food out as he laughs at me, trying desperately to maintain some sort of dignity as he sits there and covers his mouth with his hand.

"Sorry. You were asleep, but I wanted to make sure you had something to eat when you woke up." I smile back at him and take another bite of my burger, tossing him a wink as I swallow. *Wish I was swallowing something else, if you know what I mean.* I wonder if getting settled here won't be a good thing? Maybe Ronnie can finally get that fucking STD test he's so paranoid about. Lucky me, I got my blood work done at

DOLL FACE

the hospital and I'm all clean. I wonder what's the best way to bring that shit up?

"I appreciate it, really I do. You can't help that your country puts sugar in every single fucking food item, and I can't help that I love Vegemite on toast. It's just the way things fucking are."

"Please tell me you also had a pet kangaroo growing up. That'd make my day." My turn to laugh and spit bits of hamburger out on my plate. My side aches in protest and I have to clamp down on the emotion as I glare at Ronnie and try not to smile. My sister is dead; I killed somebody. A *second* somebody to be exact. I shouldn't be sitting here laughing, but I can't seem to help myself. I genuinely *like* this guy.

"I had a couple of budgies and a rainbow lorikeet, but no kangaroos. Sorry to burst your bubble. What about you? You grew up in Los Angeles, so you must've lived next to a movie star, preferably one who starred in action thrillers and toted shotguns around in their Hummer, painted a brilliant red, white, and blue, of course."

"Actually," Ronnie says, leaning back against the headboard and poking at his food with a finger. "We *did* live next to a guy who owned a Hummer. Unfortunately, it didn't have an American flag painted on it, but it *was* pretty ostentatious. I think *hummer* is a word better reserved for the bedroom." We exchange a look that heats up the room in an instant, and I sigh, setting my leftover burger back on the plate.

"I want to fuck," I admit and Ronnie laughs again. I like that I can make him smile so easily. Hopefully this is a skill that'll last. I *want* whatever this is between us to be something that really matters. "But I guess having you humping away at me would be pretty painful right now."

"Guess so," Ronnie admits, sounding at least as desperate as I feel. He reaches over and grabs my plate, stacking it on top of his and setting it on the floor. "So no humping, but … " He trails off and I take a deep breath as his gaze travels down low, coming to rest right on my snatch. *Oh yeah, baby.* "I don't know, maybe if we're gentle, a good orgasm could aid in the healing process?" I swallow hard.

"I think so," I whisper as he reaches over and turns off the light. The flickering of the TV is the only source now, a bright wash of color that highlights the tattoos on Ronnie's neck and side, his arms, his hand. So much ink to explore. I haven't gotten a single proper moment to really trace it out. I'd like to. I really, really would. I lean back and spread my legs, sighing as Ronnie scoots

DOLL FACE

between them and pushes the jersey dress out of the way. The black fabric bunches around my hips as he takes hold of my panties and strips them off, tossing them to the floor unceremoniously.

Without hesitation, he gets comfy, lying out flat on the bed, legs dangling off the end as he finds a good spot, breathing hot breath against my body. I shiver as his fingers trail down my thighs, teasing me with the softest touch of flesh on flesh. I'd give anything to have him ram me with his hard cock, fill me up, make me scream while he shot his seed inside of me. I hate to admit it, but I'm jealous, just a little, of those other women. They had Ronnie's babies, and I can't even have his bare cock. I groan as his mouth makes contact with my heat, lips pressing gently against me before I feel a sharp burst of tongue.

I lift my hands up and fist my fingers in the fabric of the pillows, squeezing tight, biting my lower lip as Ronnie switches between the soft, barely there brush of lips and tense swipes of his hot tongue. I have to actually focus on my muscles, force them to relax. If I squeeze too tight, my body responds with a white hot burst of pain that curls my toes – and not in a good way.

I let out a long breath, letting my body melt into the sheets, enjoying the feel of Ronnie's hands as he takes hold of my hips and pulls me a little closer. He takes his time pleasuring me, and I've got to admit – I'm amazed. I haven't known many guys in my life that would be so eager to go down on a girl, particularly with the knowledge that they wouldn't be getting anything in return. *Fuck.* I don't deserve this, any of this. I'm a fucking *murderer* for fuck's sake. While I can convince myself that killing Joel was an act of self-defense, I have no excuse for the roadie girl, Marta. I might not have struck the final blow, but I was there, and I helped. Nobody can ever forgive me for that.

I feel my body tensing again and have to force my muscles to relax, letting my mind drift away to a pleasantly neutral space. The only emotion I allow in when I take my next breath is the love I feel for Ronnie. It's brand new, just a little sprout, but I know if I nurture it, it'll turn into something bigger, better than I ever could've imagined.

Little spirals of pleasure swirl through my body, starting down below where Ronnie's mouth brushes my swollen flesh, and climbing upward until his touch is like a drug I can't get enough of. I force myself to breathe slowly, fighting my body's natural inclination to start panting. My muscles relax one by one, coming undone and laying me open and bare for only Ronnie to see. I let my fingers curl into the pillow next to me before I drag it over my head and bite down, draining the last of my tension out through my jaw. I want to beg him to fuck me – no, to *make love* to me – but I can't. Seriously, I got *shot* last week. My body promises that I give two shits less than none, but I manage to keep quiet, pressing the clean cotton fabric into my mouth as a shiver washes through me. Like any good drummer, Ronnie can read the rhythm in my body and knows exactly where to put his sticks – or in this case, *fingers*. He slides them into me like he's starting a new song on set, nice and slow, warming up the crowd for some grand finale. Only this time, the only person Ronnie's playing for is little old me.

I moan and it turns into a sigh as I drag the pillow away and toss it to the floor, lifting my head just a bit to stare at Ronnie, to see him buried between my legs, shirtless and beautiful. I grab a hold of his dark hair, still damp from the shower, and squeeze tight, pressing him down with a fluttering of my lashes and another sigh. When his tongue circles my clit, I feel my spine arch and my grip tighten. One more, brilliant little lick later and I'm groaning and collapsing into the pillows, shuddering as a wave of contentment washes over me and the orgasm kicks my ass to the curb, draining my energy in the best way possible.

"Bloody hell, fuckface," I whisper as Ronnie climbs up beside me and crosses his arms on the pillow, gazing at me with his beautiful brown eyes. I roll over and lift my face up for a kiss, tasting the wetness of my own body on Ronnie's full lips. "Mmm, that was nice," I murmur, "a little tame, but nice." He laughs at me and reaches up to ruffle my hair, and my heart skips a beat.

"Tame is all you get until you've healed up a bit. There's no way in fuck I'm flipping your ass over a counter for at least another two weeks." I make a pouty face, but it quickly morphs into a yawn as I lay back and let my eyes close. The TV's still on, flickering brightly. I can hear people screaming at each other, probably about some worthless drama that won't mean shit in a week or two. If they only knew the half of what we'd been through, they'd stop their whinin' and carrying on about who screwed who or who stole whose half-eaten sandwich out of the fridge. *God, I love reality TV.*

I feel an orgasm laden smile flicker across my lips as Ronnie's fingers slide through my hair and his lips brush against mine. There's no tongue, just a gentle brushing of his flesh against mine. I sigh again, a strange feeling of joy bubbling in my chest. Sure, my sister's dead and my life's gone to shit, but this could be good right here, real good, something to take away the pain without a needle or a bottle of vodka. This whole love thing could work out really well for me.

Provided, of course, that I don't get shot again. Think I've had enough of that, thank you very much.

I snap to with a start, expecting shit to rain down from the sky at any moment. My breath is heaving and my body's cursing my ass for letting the painkillers wear off. With a groan, I drop a hand to my belly and glance up to find Ronnie standing next to the food cart, looking back at me with concern in his brown eyes. He sets a silver lid down on a steaming pile of pancakes and moves over to me, kneeling down next to the bed and brushing some hair away from my face.

"You alright, doll face?" he asks me and I nod, swallowing hard and forcing myself past the wave of dread and pain that rolls over me. Yeah, getting shot sucked. So did losing me sister. Oh, and don't forget the fact that I have no band now, no career, no place to call my own. But it's over. It's over and that is a *good* thing.

I swallow again and suck in a deep breath, trying to find my words. For weeks now, I've woken up everyday with my stomach in knots and a thick, heavy layer of melancholia slathered across my soul. Today is … different. Still painful but different. That's a good thing.

"Spectacular," I grind out as he helps me sit up and I lean into the headboard with a sigh. "I could use a few pills and a durry though." Ronnie raises an eyebrow and I lean over to press a kiss to his lips. "A fag. A cigarette. A smoke."

"Gotcha," he says, returning the kiss and rising to his feet. Unfortunately, the asshole's found time to not only get up and order us breakfast, but also to put on a shirt. *Damn.* I was really enjoying the view. Ronnie grabs my pills and a cup of ice water from the tray, peeling off a layer of plastic that's stuck to the top of the cup – fucking weird ass room service shit – and then brings them both over to me. After he hands them off and I swallow several more of the little white pills than I probably should, Ronnie fishes a pack of cigs from his pocket and lights one up for me, taking a drag before passing it over. "Milo already called twice to remind me that this is a non-smoking hotel," he says with a smile as I put the white stick between my lips and wink up at him. "But I'll just remind him all the shit you've been through if he

DOLL FACE

complains. If we can afford a multi-million dollar mansion, I guess we can pay the two hundred dollar cleaning deposit."

"You sure this is okay?" I ask, taking a deep drag and letting the smoke fuck my lungs with happy tobacco kisses before I sigh and gesture randomly with the cigarette. "I mean, me living with you assholes and all. I don't want to cramp anyone's style."

"Lola, baby, you *are* my style," Ronnie says as he grabs a silver tray and sets it down on my lap. "If anything, *I'm* the one who's going to be putting a damper on all the fun." He sits down on the edge of the bed and turns away from me, voice dropping a notch. There's something there, threaded through his words, a strangeness I'm not used to hearing. Is that ... *fear* that I'm sensing? What the fuck could Ronnie be afraid about in regards to yours truly? If I look at it anyway but sideways, it seems *I'm* the one who should be grateful to him. "I ... didn't know when or how I was going to bring this up, but I guess now's as good a time as any." Ronnie clears his throat and turns back to me, running his hands down the front of his white T-shirt. It has a wolf engulfed in flames, snarling at me from the black and orange print. I try to focus on that as I take another drag of the cigarette.

"Whatever this confession is, Ronnie, it's not going to gut me, is it?" I flick my gaze up to his and find it pleading. *Crap.* He's like a Goddamn puppy dog, only one that's big and brutish but still cute. Like a pit bull or something. I feel my mouth twitch.

"I have to take responsibility for the things I've done." My stomach clenches and the skin around my wound pinches, giving me a sharp bite of pain that makes my nose wrinkle. If there's anybody in this room that needs to take responsibility, it's me. It's partially my fault that his babies lost their mothers. I *knew* and I didn't do a damn thing about it. "I have two daughters that need me more than ever." He pauses and takes a deep breath. "Okay, really, all four of my kids need me, but Lydia and Phoebe more than anyone are going to need a stable life and … a parent." Ronnie coughs again and shakes his head. I can see his hands trembling as he fists them into the comforter. At first, I think maybe he's off his guts, like he's been slammin' dope in the bathroom or something, but then I realize that that's not it all. He's just upset. I take another drag and look away, towards the food cart and not at him.

"But Lydia and Phoebe, I can't leave them with their grandparents. As soon as we get settled into the mansion … " Ronnie pauses and a chuckle warms his words. I look back over at him and feel a tiny smile tease my lips. "That sounds so Goddamn ridiculous, doesn't it? *Into the mansion.* Wow. How did I get here again?"

"You play bloody brilliant music." I cut myself off before I can add *and I helped a madman fuck you over, while we all got played by a madwoman.* "You deserve this," I say, and I mean it. I really do. "Ronnie, your daughters, are you sure you're comfortable with them being around someone like me?" I ask, dreading the answer to that question. Ronnie lifts his head and turns slowly to look at me, an expression of bafflement on his face.

"Lola," he says, struggling to find the right words. Ronnie runs a hand through his dark hair. "You're twenty-two years old, talented, gorgeous. What are you even talking about? My kids would be lucky to have someone like you in their lives. Fuck, I'd be … beyond lucky to have you in mine." His voice trails off and he looks away, squeezing his eyes shut, rubbing at his temple with his fingers, the ones with 'V' and 'E' inked on them. "I don't even feel right asking this of you, but … I have to take care of my kids." He licks his lower lip and drops his hand to his lap. "And I feel like I need you here with me." Ronnie stands up and turns to face me, reaching out and snagging my cigarette. He puts it out in an empty glass and lights up another one, putting it between his lips as he turns towards the windows. The curtains have been pulled back and California sunshine is spilling through, dripping across the carpet in golden bars. "I fucking can't even believe I'm doing this because we don't *really* know each other, but … " Ronnie blows silver smoke into the air and shakes his head. His snake tattoos draw my eyes, the brightness of the reptiles a stark contrast against his pale skin. Now that's he laid off the drugs for a while, it's got some color to it, but I guess underneath all that pastiness, he's still a white guy.

I smile a little and he sees the expression, his own softening in response.

"But you want to be with me?" I ask, hoping beyond all reason that that's true. "It's bloody fucking ridiculous, but I … I feel it, too." I cringe and shake my head, putting my hands up to my face. "Ugh, this is why I always say no to drummers." I drop my hands and point at Ronnie. "Y'hear me, mate? You fuckers are too intense."

"Lola." My name drips from Ronnie's lips like a smoldering ember, and I have to really dig my fingers into the sheets to keep still. If I throw myself in his arms and blood comes squirtin' out my side, it could very well ruin what's turning into an awkward but somewhat

DOLL FACE

pleasant moment. "I had love once. Hard-core, drop everything for this and run, true fucking love. I had it, and I lost it." His voice starts to quiver, and I feel my own eyes watering. I know all about Ronnie's lost love. I had to research his life as part of my 'mission'. Fuck. What a lousy, cock sucking piece of shit I am. "Asuka Maebara. I thought she was the only woman I could ever love, but I think ... no, I *know* that you have that same spark for me, Lola." Ronnie moves back over to the bed and reaches down to grab my chin in gentle fingers, drawing my gaze back to his. "You're my second chance, Lola. My *only* chance. If it's not you, then it's nobody. But if I have to wait, until my kids are grown or until you're ready or what the fuck ever, I will. I will *wait* for you."

"Don't be stupid," I snort, but I can feel my eyes watering again. "You don't have to wait for shit. I'm here, Ronnie, and this is where I intend to stay. If you'll have me, of course."

I keep my gaze to the side, focusing on the windows instead of his face, but I can *feel* his smile like a pleasant warmth spreading across my skin. His fingers slide along my jaw and weave through my hair, tugging my head gently against his belly.

"Lola, I'd do anything to have you by my side, I hope

you know that." Ronnie pauses and takes a deep breath. "To tell you the truth, I'm scared."

I pull away and look up at him as he drops his hands by his sides and gives me a sad smile.

"About what?" I ask, my voice as soft as the yellow sunshine on the carpet. This moment's getting emotional, and I don't do emotional particularly well. I swallow hard and close my eyes, taking a breath that mimics Ronnie's.

"My daughters. My parents. My life. Lola, I've been out of commission for a decade. The last ten years are nothing but fuzzy memories blurred into the sides of my brains. I haven't been sober since Asuka died, haven't even been coherent since Travis. I don't know how to be an adult, how to make decisions. Fuck, I don't even know how to function outside of the band." I meet Ronnie's brown eyes and watch the flickering of pain that crashes through his irises. "But if you're here, with me, we can get through this. I know we can."

I snort and try not to let him see that his emotional rambling is actually having an effect on me. *For fuck's sake, this Hallmark greeting card shit makes me weepy.* I run my hands down my face just so I can hide the slight shimmer of tears.

DOLL FACE

"There you go again," I tell Ronnie, fingertips resting on my lips as I mumble at him, "giving me that intense drummer stare, that dedication that I don't deserve. I killed your daughters' mums. I don't even deserve to play that role."

"Lola." Ronnie's voice is firm now as he sits beside me and rests a hand on my knee. "You didn't pull the trigger, didn't set this whole mess up, didn't start a fucking war by murdering the biological father of your child and then fucking with the head of the sociopath who raised him. To me, you're as much a victim here as anyone." I shake my head, but Ronnie's having none of my shit today. "For the last few weeks, I've watched you spiral down into a depression that I recognize far too well. I've been intimate with despair for a good third of my life." He reaches out and takes my hands in his, running his thumbs over my knuckles. "Let's make today day one of our new life. I can't say for sure that all this shit is behind us, and I know you're not going to just forget your sister ever existed, but I think if we try really fucking hard, we can make shit happen."

I bite my tongue to keep the fucking monster monsoon of tears at bay and turn towards Ronnie, leaning in for a kiss that pleases more than just the bits down under, but makes my heart shiver a little. Am I afraid? Fuck yes,

I'm bloody Goddamn terrified. But I'm also excited. It's a small spark, but like that sprout of love I feel for Ronnie in my heart, I know if I fan this one, I can turn it into a raging flame.

I snuggle closer and pause as the door bursts open and Turner Campbell appears, hands on his hips, chin raised in defiant glee. *Fucking fuck. If we have to live with this asshole, we're getting triple locks on our door and a Do Not Disturb sign written in blood.*

"Get your shit together. We're meeting the owner of the house we just bought. She's giving us the keys and letting us live there until closing. Only thing we have to pay her with are some autographs and shit." Turner snaps his fingers. "Hop to it, bitches. This shit is prompt. Get ready and don't skimp on the eyeliner." Turner slams the door behind him while Ronnie and I exchange another look.

"Beverly Hills, huh?" I ask and Ronnie sighs, but not like he's upset, just ... anxious. We all are, I think. "Everyone's going to think I'm away with the pixies when I tell them where I'm living."

"Do you have any idea how much the mortgage payment on this baby's going to be?" Ronnie asks and I raise an eyebrow. "It's five digits long, I'll tell you that much." He shakes his head and chuckles, rising to his feet and moving to the window. When Ronnie glances over his shoulder at me, he's smiling. "Somehow, I have a good feeling about this though. I don't know how or why, but I've been numb to my senses for too long. I think that this time, I'm going to listen."

"I think that sounds like a good idea, Ronnie," I say, pushing myself to my feet and closing my eyes against a wave of dizziness. I move over to stand next to him and stare out at the bustling nightmare that is Los Angeles. We're a long way from fucking Giru, Queensland, aren't we? I curl my fingers around the windowsill as a thought comes to mind. "Fuck a duck," I growl as my nails dig into the white paint. Ronnie glances over at me and I look back at him. "When I came to the states, I just said I was here on holiday."

"What are you saying?" Ronnie asks with a raised eyebrow. "That you're going to get deported? Back to Australia? Does that even happen?" He runs a hand through his hair and shakes his head. "Um, okay. We can fix this, I'm sure. I ... " Ronnie pauses, like he's just thought of something. I keep staring at him, waiting for an answer to this problem. I shouldn't be surprised by what he says, but I am anyway. "Maybe we should ... " He swallows hard and scratches at the snake tattoos around his neck, letting his beautiful brown eyes slide over to me as his mouth twitches. "Lola, maybe we should get hitched?"

CHAPTER 8
Ronnie McGuire

"So you, like, said *marry me and I'll get ya a green card*? That's super hot. I'm sure Lola pissed her pants in eagerness to accept that shit." Turner lights up a cigarette and blows smoke at my face. I scowl at him and snatch my lighter back, enjoying the privacy of our new pad. Getting out of the hotel was a Goddamn nightmare – despite Milo's best efforts, they found us again and the swarm this time was *epic*. Based on the turnout, I have a feeling making that five figure fucking mortgage payment isn't going to be a problem. "Wait, wait," he continues, taking another drag, "lemme guess. She was all *'Crikey, mate! That's bloody brilliant. Let's throw*

some shrimp on the barbie to celebrate.'"

"Your faux Australian accent is almost as bad as your Irish one – almost. And I'm pretty sure most people would find you ridiculously offensive." I light up and tuck the lighter in my pants pocket. "Hell, *I* find you ridiculously offensive and we've been friends for-fucking-ever. Cool it, Arkansas, and keep your idiosyncrasies to yourself." Turner scowls at me and flicks hot ash in my direction. "If you really did propose to Naomi – and I'm not passing judgment on that until she wakes up and tells me herself – then I doubt it was any smoother. In fact, I'd bet one of our mammoth mortgage payments that it was worse."

"Yeah? Well, fuck you. You have too many kids. Get a fucking vasectomy before you get Lola pregnant." I shake my head and look up at the brilliant blue of the sky. Speaking of, I *really* need to get tested. I mean, like, sooner rather than later.

"Let's make an appointment," I say to Turner while we wait for the owner and her real estate agent to arrive. "Let's go get tested."

"Tested?" Turner asks, recoiling with a strange expression on his face. "For what?"

"STIs," I say and then sigh when he continues with

the look of sheer bafflement. "Sexually transmitted infections."

"What the fuck are you trying to say, man?" Turner growls, flicking his cigarette to the driveway and crushing it out with his boot. I notice Camby, the Barbie perfect real estate agent, cringe in the background. "That I'm, like, fucking diseased or some shit? I never forget to bring balloons to the party. You're the one that's always ramming chicks bareback. Go get your junk fondled by some doctor and prepare to see it on the front page of every news website in existence."

"If you're even half as serious about Naomi as I am about Lola, you'll come with me and get checked out." Turner looks away at the mention of Amatory Riot's lead singer and flicks his tongue across his lower lip in nervousness. As of an hour ago, Naomi's condition hadn't changed. Turner freaked the fuck out over that, but I think at this point, no news is good news. At least she's not getting worse. I look up at the sky again and wish I had a God I trusted that I could pray to.

"Fine. Whatever. But I bet you're the only one of us with anything. Hopefully you don't have the herp."

"The … herp?" I ask, raising an eyebrow at my friend.

"Yeah, the herp," Trey says, rolling up his wheelchair

to sit beside us. I was with Lola last night, so I didn't get to be there when Turner delivered the news about the mansion, but Jesse and Treyjan have always been on whatever train Turner's intent on riding. If he's happy, they're happy. End of story. "Herpes. You have herpes, dude?"

"Herpes?" I jump and turn to find Lola staring at me with wide eyes and an open mouth. "Oh, fuck, Ronnie. If you gave me that shit, I will *job* your arse." I hold up my hands in a placating gesture and let my cigarette hang loosely from my lips.

"Okay, fuck, that I *know* I don't have. I was just saying it's always good to get tested. Jesus." Lola breathes a sigh of relief, leaning against the car and taking deep breaths. I tried to get her to use the wheelchair, but she wouldn't do it. Too much pride. I feel a smile creep over my lips. After I essentially asked her to marry me, she got red faced and started sputtering. I have no idea what to make of that, but I can promise if somebody tries to ship my new lady overseas, there could very well be a shirtless ass kicking.

We all pause and turn as a pair of cars pulls through the gates and comes to a stop behind our rented van. I guess if we're going to be hanging around L.A. for awhile, I'm going to have to buy something to drive.

DOLL FACE

Hmm. I wonder briefly about our buses, still stuck back in Oklahoma City. Wonder when we'll be getting those back and what we're going to do with them once we do. Next time we tour, we're going to have to change up our travel pattern a little. I shudder at the thought. It's going to take some time to get comfortable with the idea again.

I lean back and cross my arms over my chest, waiting as people pile out of the two cars. I dressed in my best, in an Amatory Riot T-shirt with no holes, a pair of new jeans that Milo found time to shove in my bag God only knows when. Hair's done, eyeliner's on, face is shaved. We're all good to go.

A curvy brunette appears from the backseat of one of the vehicles, dark hair shining in the sunlight. Her navy skirt suit and confident smirk give me the distinct impression that *she* is the current owner of this house. What she does or where she's from, I'm not sure, but to afford a place like this, she must be badass.

"Good morning everyone," she says, sweeping her hands down the front of her perfect suit and smiling a perfect Beverly Hills smile – all cosmetic sterility and disingenuousness. I follow the swing of her gaze as she skips over Josh, arms crossed and scowling near our rented van, to Jesse, Trey, Turner, and then finally coming to rest on my face. I drop my cigarette and crush it out while she stares at me, brown eyes sparkling. She's a beautiful woman but I can see from the neutral shade of her eyeshadow, the conservative cut of her skirt, the pale almond color of her hair, all of it is meant to de-sexualize her, give her a more average sort of a look. I'm immediately on my guard. The only other person I've met in my life like this was America Harding.

I grit my teeth and cross my arms over my chest.

"Hey baby," Turner says, flipping the charm switch to high. He must *really* want this fucking house. Brunette lady drags her gaze from me and back to my friend, switching up her dazzling white grin to the next level.

"Let me just be the first to say that you gentlemen have excellent taste in real estate." Turner lifts his chin with a smirk while I get out another cigarette and roll my eyes. This chick's bad news. I can tell already that whatever it is she's selling, I'm not buying. I look over at Lola, arms crossed over her chest and face pale. I need to get her to sit down and relax, have a fucking lemonade or something. "It's an honor to be able to meet with you in private like this. If you don't mind, I have a few little souvenirs I'd *love* for you to sign. Oh!" Brunette Lady grins and clasps her hands together. "I've forgotten to introduce myself. How silly." She flips her hair and moves up to me, offering her hand and locking gazes.

DOLL FACE

She knows I'm not buying her shit. Great.

I reach out and shake with her.

"Paulette Washington," she says and warning bells go off in my head. I squeeze her hand tight and let go, taking a step back.

"Paulette Washington, like the TV producer?" I ask, raising an eyebrow as her smile ratchets up yet another notch. *Huh.* Didn't even think that was possible. *I fucking hate California. Why did we even come back here?* I take another drag on my cigarette and watch her carefully as she moves down the line and then comes back to Turner, dropping some keys into the palm of his hand before answering me.

"Keys to the kingdom, my friend," she says and then levels her gaze on me again. "And yes, Ronnie, I'm flattered." She touches a hand to her chest like she's not at all surprised. She *wanted* one of us to recognize her. In fact, she was *counting* on it. I was feeling suspicious about this whole transaction. I mean, it's not *unheard* of for a seller to let her buyers rent out the place before closing, but it's not usually this easy. Now I get it. This bitch wants something from us – something besides a few selfies and some swag. "In fact, I was thinking while we were all gathered here that I might discuss an idea I had with you.

Milo steps forward and straightens his pale pink tie, getting ready to step in and take control when Turner opens his big, fat mouth.

"TV producer? Huh? What shows you work on?" he asks and Paulette's eyes sparkle with triumph.

"Come inside," she says and then pauses with a false laugh that makes my teeth hurt. *Aw, man. We just got rid of one fake bitch, the last thing we need is another.* Unfortunately for us, we're in Beverly Hills. That's pretty much what the entire city is populated with. "I mean, it's *your* house now, so if that's okay?" Turner shrugs before I get a chance to protest and spins on his heel, glancing up at the imposing facade of our new place with a sniffle of approval.

"Be my guest, doll," he says before disappearing up the front steps and into the house. The rest of my band files after him and I watch as Jesse and Josh lift Trey's wheelchair up the few stairs and into the foyer. A series of wild curses follows as Treyjan gets his first look at the place and I stand there, watching the interaction between the realtors and Paulette. Six big burly dudes stand in the background and I have a hard time remembering which ones are ours and which ones came with Paulette.

DOLL FACE

Apparently it's not just Brayden Ryker who has blank-faced, unmemorable bodyguards. I make a note to try to find some distinguishing features on our guys.

"I don't much like this woman," Lola says, keeping her position against the car next to me. I turn slowly and catch her blue-eyed gaze. "That bitch has got tickets on herself." Lola pulls out a cigarette and lights up, smiling at my raised eyebrows. "She's so fucking full of herself, looks like she's about to burst out of that perfect suit of hers."

"I agree," I say with a sigh, running my hands down my face. "So I better get in there and make sure shit doesn't go South faster than a flock of fucking geese." I drop my hands and try to smile at Lola. I keep expecting there to be some weirdness between us after this morning's conversation, but I don't feel anything but hope when I look at her. Good sign, right? Still, I better bring up that whole botched marriage proposal shit before it bites me in the ass. We're not ready for that yet, but if that's what we gotta do to keep her here with me, then that's what we're gonna fucking do. Provided, of course, that that's what Lola wants.

I hold out my hand and she takes it, a little unsteady on her feet. But we don't rush, we move across the gray brick pavers towards the front steps and climb them one at a time. I can already hear Paulette's authoritative boom echoing around the immaculately decorated mansion. *I can't even believe I agreed to this,* I think as Lola takes a look around and shakes her head in disbelief.

"Can't tell if this is a fairy fucking tale or a nightmare," she says under her breath as we pause in the doorway to the living room and my eyes catch on the walnut woodwork crisscrossing the ceiling. Turner's sprawled out in a high backed chair, its gaudy gold fabric a strange contrast against his holey black jeans and blue T-shirt. This one says *I'm Taken, Bitches.* How appropriate.

"Think of it like this," Paulette's saying, completely and utterly ignoring our manager as he tries to get a word in edgewise. She lifts her flawless hand up and spreads her long fingers as she gestures absently towards me and Lola. "Five of rock's most eligible bachelors, living in one house. Real life, real drama, real music. What do you think? You're the next big thing, Mr. Campbell." My best friend frowns, and I can tell this is about to get real ugly up in here. *Crap.*

"First off, we're not bachelors. I'm engaged." Turner pauses and glances over at me as Paulette's face shifts from professional but excited to outright fucking gleeful. "And Ronnie over here, he's engaged." He nods his chin at me, and I cringe. I can't look at Lola right now. Frankly, I'm terrified to see the expression on her face. "And second," he says, digging the hole even deeper. Milo, bless his fucking heart, tries to stop him but there's no stopping Turner Campbell once he gets started. "I'm not the *next* big thing. I *am* the biggest fucking thing there ever was." He snorts and sits up, leaning towards Paulette with a smile stretching across his face. "But I'm also listening. You want to make a show about us? I think that's a perfect frigging idea."

"Turner," I say, but Josh jumps in first from his spot on the nearby love seat. "I am *not* fucking living here." He turns to Paulette, sweeping blonde hair away from his face. "I am not living here. Look, Milo begged me to come over, so I could sign whatever it was you wanted signed and the guys could get their keys. I mean, we're not even really *friends*."

"Shut the fuck up, Josh," Turner says, kicking the corner of the sofa. "Weren't you complaining on the way over that your parents couldn't even go to work without getting swarmed by the paparazzi? How fair is it for you to be staying with them when you can't even step into the backyard without people leaping over the fence at your ass? Keep your mouth closed and know a good thing when you see it."

I help Lola over to the love seat and Josh scoots over a cushion, so she can sit down. As soon as she does, Paulette's eyes swing her direction.

"So you and Ronnie are engaged then?" she asks, and I feel the blood drain from my face. I flip Turner the bird and try to intervene in the situation before it gets much worse.

"Don't see how that's any of your business," Lola says, blowing smoke in Paulette's face. The woman doesn't even so much as blink. Her brown eyes remain calm and focused and her hands lay folded in her lap.

"Just think about this, boys," she says, ignoring Milo and turning her attention to Treyjan, still stuck in his wheelchair, face pale, and chest heaving. He should be resting and not dealing with this shit. "A reality TV show that's actually *reality*, your reality. I mean, you tell me, Treyjan, what it's like, going from an abused young boy in a trailer park to a man whose band may very well be the first in recent history to outsell Michael Jackson's *Thriller*?" As usual, Trey looks to Turner for what to say and the two of them exchange a look.

"I, uh, I didn't know we'd sold that many copies," he blurts and Paulette throws her head back in laugher, giving Milo an appraising look and a strange smile. She points her finger at him, her nude nail polish shimmering in the sprinkle of afternoon sunshine leaking in from the backyard.

"Oh, you're good. Too good, maybe." Paulette rises to her feet, surprising me as she grabs her purse and swings it over her shoulder. Her gaze pans around the room, oblivious to the intricate details all around us, the ones that have got Jesse mesmerized. This place really *is* a fucking palace. "Well, you've heard what I had to say. Now wait until you see what the studio is willing to pay you for the deal. I'll send you an email, Mr. Terrabotti, with some of the details and maybe we can have lunch?" Without waiting for an answer, Paulette turns away, dragging her bodyguards with her. She pauses near the front door and glances over her shoulder. "Nice to meet you all. I hope you enjoy the house. My husband had it custom built, spared no expense." She tosses us a wink and disappears, just like that. I think we're all too stunned to think of anything to say. After all, we might be 'rock stars' now, maybe you'd even call us 'celebrities', but we're still just a bunch of assholes from Los Angeles who got lucky. Or unlucky. Depends on how you see it. People had to die for this fame; my friend and my lover had to get shot. I don't know. If I could go back in time, I'm not sure I'd do it all over again.

"Well, shit," Turner says, rising to his feet and looking around the room. It might be furnished, but it's sparse, just barely staged to entice buyers to cash in on this monstrosity of a house. Home. This is going to be my fucking *home* from now on. Jesus Christ. "I thought I missed our buses, but this shit is the fucking bomb." Turner tucks his hands into his jeans pockets and leans back. His posture is all cocky confidence, but his eyes tell a different story. He wishes Naomi were here. I hope for both their sakes that she wakes up sooner rather than later. The look on her face when she finds out that Turner's not only spilled their supposed engagement to a big time TV producer but also that he's purchased a mansion worth more than a small country, that's going to be priceless.

"Speaking of buses," Milo begins and we all groan. He has that no nonsense voice on, the one that brooks no argument. He always uses it to start off business discussions. "The repairs are nearly done, and I'd like to know what you boys would like to do with it. I also need to know what you want to do with the staff vehicles as well – the trailers and motor homes. My recommendation would be to sell them, but of course, it's up to you as well."

"Keep the bus, sell the rest," Turner says, waving his

DOLL FACE

hand at Milo. "You deal with the details. Right now, I don't want to talk shop. I want to wander around my new fucking house." A grin tears across his lips and his black lip rings reflect the light back at my face. "This is so much better than a single wide piece of shit with a toilet that doesn't flush and a couch that smells like piss. What do you think, Trey?"

"We've sold more albums than Michael Jackson?" Trey asks, his brown brows drawing together as he stares at his knees and lets his mouth hang open in abject shock. "How the fuck did that happen? Are we billionaires?"

"Not yet, Mr. Charell," Milo says with a tired sigh. He fixes his tie again and tries to force a smile. "But I will let you know when and if you get there." He claps his hands together and glances over at our bodyguards. "Boys, you do understand that everything is different now." Turner shrugs like he's not listening, but I nod at Milo to keep going. Sure, I'd like to check the house out, but I also know that he's right. Everything *is* different. I look down at the floor and close my eyes, listening to the sudden silence that ensues. "We need to hire more staff. I'm going to need an assistant. You're going to need lawyers, publicists, accountants. It's not just me and you anymore. Do you understand that?"

Nobody speaks, and I sigh.

C.M. Stunich

"We understand," I say, but I'm not sure that my friends do. Josh is a middle class dude who got lucky, handpicked by Milo and thrust into our mess. Turner, Trey, and Jesse are down on their luck kids with shitty pasts and no clue how to exist in the real world. This is, like, real world shit on crack. I take a breath and close my eyes. I *just* got sober. I'm *just* figuring out how to live without Asuka by my side. It almost feels like it's too much, like my body's going to break under the weight of all this stress. "We also know that we're definitely *not* fucking into doing a reality TV show. Can you imagine having cameras following us around all day? Fuck that."

"Come on, Ronnie. Don't be a Goddamn downer. At least think about it." I give Turner a look and purse my lips.

"You told that woman that Lola and I were engaged, Turner. Why the hell would you think that was okay?" He gives me a blank look, and I sigh. Getting that man to realize his own faults is damn near impossible. Seems like the only person on this earth who's capable of it is Naomi Knox. Huh. I miss her already. "And that you and Naomi were engaged. You better be telling the truth on that one, asshole. Don't mess around with Naomi. She's not the type of woman who takes shit and smiles."

Lola snorts and glances over her shoulder at me.

"Yeah, whatever," Turner growls, stalking away with Trey attempting to roll his wheelchair after him. I put out a hand and stop him, looking down with all due seriousness.

"Where's your fucking nurse?" I ask and he shrugs guiltily.

"I fired her. I didn't like her. Why does it matter? I don't even need a nurse anymore." I slap a palm to my forehead and shake my head, wondering how the hell I ended up with these idiots. Trey watches me as Turner disappears up the stairs and Jesse sighs dramatically. "Hey Ronnie," Trey says, and I feel something horrible coming my way. I look up and thank the fucking Gods that I found Lola. Without her, I don't know if I could handle this shit. "Is it ... true?"

"Is what true?" I ask as my friend's face crumbles in pain and his breath hitches violently.

"That *America* killed Travis? That she's the one that ran him over with her car?" I stare back at Trey and try to find the right words to say. I haven't given much thought to the revelations that plagued our concert. I have to find a really good, really frigging stable place in my life to go there. "Because, you know, he should be here with us right now and he's not, and that is *fucked*."

Trey sniffles and looks away for a moment before grabbing onto the wheels of his chair and dragging himself out of the living room.

I sigh and drop my hands to my sides.

Milo's giving me a sympathetic look that I'm not sure how to take in. What can I say anyway? Trey's right. This *is* fucked. Because of America – and Stephen – Lola's going to have to feel the same pain that I did when my brother was taken away from me. We might not have been related by blood, but I loved him all the same.

"Hey." I move around the couch and kneel by her side, trying to force a smile. If she's thinking at all about her sister, she doesn't let on, twisting her lips up at the corners and returning my expression. The look's a little blank, doesn't quite reach her eyes, but that's okay. I don't expect it to. The only thing that numbs pain is love. Some people think it's time, but I'm living, breathing proof that that's not always true. "You want to look around?" I nibble at my lip for a moment in thought and let my gaze catch on the intricate woodwork that lines the ceiling. I pray to some distant God of craftsmanship that Turner doesn't ruin it. "Pick out our room or whatever?"

Lola chuckles and adjusts the stretchy fabric of her dress. It's weird, seeing her in this flowing white gown.

DOLL FACE

Normally, this chick's got painted on leather pants and barely there tops. I let my eyes trace the sweetheart neckline at the top and then rise to meet her gaze.

"I haven't picked out a room since I was six and my family moved into the farmhouse." Lola runs her hands down her face and pulls them away, her smile a little more stiff this time. No doubt she really is thinking of Poppet right now. I hold out a hand and she takes it, following me to the stairs and pausing as we both gaze up at the swirling steps with trepidation. Even though I grew up dead center middle class America, I'm still a little weirded out at the grandiosity of this place. It doesn't feel right, like it's too good for me, like I don't deserve it. What have I ever done to earn this? I'm not a humanitarian. I don't rescue orphans. I didn't invent a cure for cancer. I'm just a mediocre drummer who got wrapped up in somebody else's shit.

Lola's fingers tighten around mine, like she can sense the direction of my thoughts. I squeeze back and we start up the stairs, running into Turner as we hit the second floor. His face is red and he's panting like he's run a marathon. He tries to smile at us, but he looks closer to tears than he does joy.

"This place is wicked awesome," he says, sniffling and brushing hair from his forehead. "Killer. I picked out my and Naomi's room. It's the one at the end of the hall with the black bedspread and a bathroom ten times the size of my mother's trailer." With a salute, Turner moves past us and back down the stairs, calling out for Trey.

I take a breath and pull Lola along with me, down a hallway with cream colored marble floors and metal sconces on the wall. It's all so … sterile. We're going to have to figure out a way to make this place feel like a home, all twenty-five thousand fucking square feet of it. Our footsteps sound loud against the floors, like intruders, bums breaking into the back window of an empty house for the night. I get a sudden flash of memory, a fuzzy blur of myself doing just that, getting high in the back bedroom of some poor fuck's three bedroom house. I was such a blight on suburbia after Asuka died. If it hadn't been for Travis … I might not have even *survived* that time period in my life.

"I'm feeling … overwhelmed," I whisper as Lola lets go of my hand and opens one of the many doors that border this antiseptic fucking hallway. She glances over her shoulder at me, breath coming in small spurts. Maybe I shouldn't have let her walk up those stairs?

"Ain't the only one," she whispers as she raises an eyebrow and turns back to face the extravagant splendor of the bedroom. *Holy fuck.* I run my fingers through my hair, try to take in the four poster bed, the balcony doors framed with more curtains that I've ever seen in my fucking life, a pair of couches near the *fireplace* and a bathroom door that's thankfully closed. I don't know if I could handle much more than this in one go around. "There's a bloody living room in here," Lola says, pausing in the doorway that separates the front half of the bedroom with the back. There's a pair of white doors that Lola slides experimentally from the walls with a mumbled curse under her breath. Shit. Suburbia would've worked just fine for me.

I move across the room, trying to count the dozens of footsteps that it takes me to get to the balcony and open the doors. I'm staring down at the pool now, at Turner stripping off his T-shirt and Trey sitting in his wheelchair nearby.

"This is ridiculous," I say and they both look up at me. Turner grins, but his face still holds that inner pain that I hope to fucking Christ doesn't morph into the soul drenching melancholia that I used to eat for breakfast, lunch, and dinner. "I feel like a jewelry box and a Pottery Barn fucked and had an illegitimate baby – and then it threw up this house. What the hell is all of this? Do people really live in places like this?"

Turner shrugs.

"This place is, like, ten times swankier than a Pottery Barn, Ronnie. Get used to it. You're famous now." And then he dives into the pool and I sigh, lifting my chin up and gazing across the admittedly small piece of property. The entire mansion sits on less than an acre, taking up most of it in its sprawling arms. Guess that's the price we pay for location, location, location, eh? I curl my fingers around the intricate metal bannister of the balcony and try to catch a glimpse of the street. How long until people find us here? Until they start running celebrity home tours past our front gate?

"Oh, sorry." I turn and find Josh retreating out the door. "Didn't know you guys where in here." He pauses a moment and looks at Lola, lying sprawled across the massive bed. I glance up and catch his blue eyes, gesturing him back into the room.

"Stay for a minute," I say and he swallows hard, sweeping blonde hair back from his face. He scoots past Lola like he's afraid of her and pauses next to me, looking down at Turner in his boxer shorts with a scowl. "I'm sorry about all of this," I say and Josh raises his eyebrows, blue eyes confused. Fuck. He's so young. Way too young to be dealing with all of this crap. He's not even twenty-one yet. I should've said no when Milo

DOLL FACE

presented him to us as a possible candidate for bassist. At that point in my life though, I couldn't have cared less. Hell, I can't even *remember* our first meeting. I was probably high.

The crook of my elbow throbs, remembering the sweet kiss of the needle. I have to squeeze my fingers tighter around the railing to hold back the craving. Now that we're not on tour, that we've finally gotten some answers to our questions, I feel lost. Like, what the hell am I supposed to do now? Where do I go from here? I'm not used to real life, not even one coated in candy like this. *I need to get out of here for a while.*

"How was it?" I ask, knowing Josh's parents live in a neighborhood similar to my own. "Being back home? The crowds, the feeling, everything. What was it like?" Josh sighs and leans over, folding his arms across the railing and putting his forehead against them.

"Horrible. The first day I was back, I snuck into the garage and borrowed my dad's car. I thought if I could get past the crowds on the street, I could actually find some peace and quiet. They trailed me all the way to a Burger King, and once I went inside, I couldn't get out. I locked myself in the bathroom." Josh sighs heavily, and puts all his weight against the railing. "I had to call Brayden Ryker to get me out." My blood chills.

"You called Brayden Ryker?" I ask, glancing over my shoulder to see if Lola's actually asleep or just resting. I find her blue eyes on mine, sparkling like the sea in a storm. As far as I know, nobody's actually told her who murdered her sister. According to Turner, Brayden Ryker pointed his gun at Poppet's head and pulled the trigger, just like that. I turn back around and focus on Josh as he lifts his head up to look at me.

"Yeah. I didn't know who else to call. And, I don't know, but I trust that guy." Josh shrugs and stands up, scowling again when he catches sight of Turner flipping him off from the diving board. "Go fuck yourself!" he screams and retreats back into the room, spinning in a tight circle and flopping into a crimson covered chair in the corner. He puts his feet up on the ottoman and then wrinkles his nose, dragging his black and white Converse off the expensive fabric with a grimace. "I can't say anything about the future, but I can tell you that right now, living a *normal* life or any semblance of a normal life is pretty much an impossibility." Josh sags and shakes his head, focusing his blue eyes on the floor. "I spent my entire childhood wishing I could make it big, play in a real rock band, make a shit ton of money. Now that I have … I kind of wish I hadn't." He sighs and pokes at the fleur-de-lis motif on the arm of the chair.

DOLL FACE

"Anyway, you guys were probably right to get a house here, somewhere with fucking walls and a gate. When Turner said people hopped my fence into the backyard, he wasn't kidding." Josh pauses again and looks up at Lola as she groans and forces her body into a sitting position, watching us both carefully. "If it's not too much trouble, I mean, I don't really *want* to live here or anything, but maybe I could stay for a while? Just until things cool down a bit?"

I smile and clamp my hand on Josh's shoulder.

"Of course, man. Go pick a fucking bedroom." He sighs with relief and rises to his feet, tossing a smile Lola's way and disappearing into the hallway. I watch after him and take a deep breath, gathering my courage for what I know I have to do next.

"Hey," I tell Lola, turning my attention to the world's most beautiful woman. My mind calls *traitor* and tries to bring up Asuka's smile, but I refuse to look at it. I've spent *years* fantasizing about her, years looking at old photographs. It won't do me any good to keep obsessing over my lost soul mate. All I can do is try to embrace the woman in front of me, my second chance, my redemption. I make myself smile. "I don't think I can sit around here right now. To be honest, this place is giving me the chills." I cough into my hand and take a deep breath. "Would you like to go visit my parents with me? I ... need to see Lydia." Lola stares back at me for a moment, and I consider throwing out an excuse to get her to stay here. Maybe she *shouldn't* be moving around right now, anyway?

"Yeah, yeah," she says, scooting to the edge of the bed with a considerable amount of effort. I move over and take her hands in mine. I *know* we're moving too fast, that meeting the parents and dealing with the kids is usually something that comes six months or more down the line, but we're way past that now. Besides, I've learned my lesson. Time isn't always kind to love. You never know when it's just minutes and hours that you have left, instead of years. The day Asuka died, I was fantasizing about how I was going to propose to her after a year or two of college. Fucking laughable. "You know I'm always up for a bit of family drama, Ronnie," she says as I pull her to my feet and fold her gently into my arms with a sigh.

"I'm glad you are, babe," I say as I stare out the window at the foliage blowing in the gentle California breeze. "Because I'm not sure that I am."

DOLL FACE

✗ ✗ ✗

It takes a hell of a lot more maneuvering to get out of the mansion than I thought. Milo has to call in a few extra guards from the new security firm he's working with. They bring their own van, this one a hell of a lot nicer than the one we had rented before. The seats are leather and there's a pair of TVs flickering from the headrests in front of us. Champagne is served and I'm pretty sure Lola drinks an entire bottle by herself.

"Beverly Hills," I say with a sigh, and the exclamation is not one of fondness. *I hate this fucking town.* But this is where I need to be right now. I can *feel* it. As we head towards my parents' place, we pass the intersection where Asuka lost her life and a wave of pain washes over me, making me sick to my stomach. My fingers twitch and I thank fucking God that I don't have anything good on me. If I did, I'd take it.

Lola notices my shaking hands and my bouncing knee and leans over, brushing hair from my forehead.

"You alright there, mate?" she asks and I sigh, squeezing her knee and trying not to let the emotions cut me into those same grooves they've always run through. Instead, I try to focus on Lola's voice, on the conversation I had with my mom before getting in the van. When I said I was coming over, I thought she was going to have a heart attack. Other than our brief encounter at the airport, I haven't seen my parents in four years. I took her sobbing as proof that she really was excited to see me. Wait till she hears I'm planning on taking Lydia away. That oughta be exciting.

I lean my forehead against Lola's.

"We just passed the spot where Asuka breathed her last breaths," I whisper and Lola's body stiffens for a moment before she wraps her arms around me and holds on tight. We stay that way until we pull into my parents' driveway and straight into the garage where my father's waiting. He closes the door before the engine's even off and stands near the open doorway to the backyard with his arms crossed over his chest.

Fuck.

Every time I see that man's face – stern but not mean, confident but not cocky, loving without showing a hint of weakness – I feel like a little kid again. God, what a disappointment I must be for him. I'm *nothing* like the boy he raised, the one he nurtured and encouraged,

DOLL FACE

punished with compassion, believed in. *Shit. Shit. Shit.* I pull away from Lola and feel my quivers turn into full on shakes, like I'm on a frigging comedown. Great. Awesome. First time in my life that I'm not high as a freaking kite and it sure as hell looks like it.

Don't be afraid of your father, Ronnie. He loves you almost as much as I do. I can see Asuka speaking to me, winking at me, wrapping her arms around my neck. Home for five minutes and my newfound sanity's already turning to ice and cracking around me. Shards fall to my feet, melt across my skin and turn to sweat as I run my tongue over my lower lip and try to force myself out the open door. One of our security guards is standing there, off to the side, not even looking at me. The perfect celebrity escort. *Ugh.*

I feel bile rise in my throat – I can fucking *taste* that shit – as I try to pull some semblance of self-control over me, wear it like a coat in winter, protect me against the icy shards of my crumbling soul. *Oh my God.* I start to pant and feel Lola's fingers curling around mine, tugging on my hands, drawing my attention to her face.

"Ronnie," she says, voice low, blue eyes rife with concern. Her sister just died and here I am, freaking the fuck out over nothing. I'm such an asshole. "You're having a panic attack," she tells me calmly, squeezing hard, digging her thumb nails into the backs of my hands. I try to focus on her face, but images assault my mind, twisting me into a big, sweaty mass of *nothing*. A decade of believing that was true, losing the will to live, it took its toll on me. Right now, I'm paying the fucking price with hefty interest. "Breathe for me, baby," she continues, leaning her forehead against mine, sucking in a massive breath that I do my best to imitate. "You can get through this. Chin up, love." She leans back and presses her full lips against my sweaty skin, sliding her hands from mine and placing them on either side of my face. Lola's eyes are big and round, like marbles, stuck in that perfect face. They draw me in, and I let them, matching my breaths to hers.

It's not perfect, but it'll do. It'll have to.

"Son, are you alright?" My father's standing right behind me, the wisdom of his years tinting his voice with this be-all, end-all authority that turns my bones to jelly. I might be twenty-eight years old, but he's sixty-five and far wiser than me. I'm intimidated; I won't lie about that. So when I turn and have to look this guy in the face, I'm sure there's sweat dripping down the sides of my face.

"We drove past the spot where Asuka … " It seems like as good an excuse as any. The skin around my father's mouth tightens, but he nods his head like he

DOLL FACE

understands. I study him carefully, his brown eyes, his gray hair, the strong set of his shoulders. We stay like that for several moments, observing one another, taking each other's measures. I come away like I always do, feeling as if I've failed this man somehow, wasted a good portion of his life with my fuckups. I don't know what he sees in me, but he reaches out a hand to help me – and then Lola – out of the van. "Dad, this is Lola Rubi Saints. Lola, this is my father, Ronald McGuire, the first." I pause and look between the two of them as they shake hands. Lola grips tight which is good. My dad is old fashioned, judges people by their handshakes.

"Nice to meet you, Miss Saints," my father says, his expression difficult to read. The wrinkles around his eyes don't change nor does his stiff stance. He doesn't embrace me or even throw out a smile, but he's standing here and that's all that counts. After all the crap I've pulled, I wouldn't be surprised if he were to disown me. Four kids. Four different mothers. A total screwup. "Your mother's in the living room with Lydia," he says and then hesitates, like there's something he wants to ask but is afraid to. After a moment, he shakes his head, gives the bodyguards a strange look and then leads us out the back door and down a white gravel pathway in the backyard.

C.M. Stunich

The foliage is nice, the grass green, a beautiful facade of luxury and greenery plastered over a Goddamn desert. I ignore it and hold Lola's hand, moving slowly and watching her for any sign of weakness. Bringing her here was selfish, I know that. I should have left her back at the mansion to sleep. *Fuck, Ronnie, get yourself together, asshole.*

Our bodyguards trail behind us, like shadows, blotting out the brightness of the sun. I kind of wish I'd told 'em to fuck off and took my chances. I have a feeling this Stephen/America bullshit is over, at least for the most part. No more snipers, no more ruined concerts, no more bloodshed. But, hey, I guess if some crazy ass fangirls hop the fence and try to rape me, these guys can hold them off. Huh. I shake my head and run my fingers through my hair, dragging it away from my face.

My dad opens the back door of the house and leads the way into the breakfast nook and kitchen area, the cream colored granite of the countertops shimmering in the sun. As usual, everything's immaculate and homey, like a page torn from *Better Homes and Gardens*. I take a deep breath and close my eyes. Even when I was a little kid, like real real little, and my parents lived two blocks away from Turner's trailer park, everything was still nice like this. My mom put everything she had into turning that shit hole into a proper home, and it paid off. I never knew we were poor until we weren't anymore.

"Ronnie," my dad says, glancing back at the guards and gritting his teeth. I peer over my shoulder with a grimace. "Lydia hasn't been in the best place since you left her with us. She's getting better, but I think it'd be wise to introduce as little trauma as possible. Do you think your friends would mind hanging out in the kitchen for a while?"

"Yeah," I say, and one of the two men nods, stepping back near the door like he's invisible in his perfect suit and sunglasses. Jesus Christ. Where did Milo get these guys? They're nothing at all like Brayden Ryker's men – rough, wicked normal, unassuming. Our new dudes might be plain in the face, but they've got that polished Hollywood look that bugs me. Whatever. No time to deal with that right now. "They'll wait here." I turn back and nod my chin. My dad sighs, like he's regretting the decision to let me come over, and leads Lola and me into the living room.

As soon as I see Lydia, my throat gets tight and I feel my world collapsing in on itself.

She's sitting on the rug in a blue and white striped dress, playing with some of my old Hot Wheels die-cast cars. My mom sits beside her on the floor, fingering a string of pearls around her neck. She looks up when we walk in and tears fill her brown eyes.

"Ronnie," she whispers, drawing Lydia's attention around. As soon as she sees me, her face breaks into a smile. A *smile*. My knees go weak, and I suddenly find myself crouching on the hardwood floor, unable to take another step. My breath rushes out of me, and I have to close my eyes as my mother rises to her feet and moves towards me. I manage to stand up in time to see Lydia climbing to her feet and following after, wrapping her hand in my mother's dress. "It's so good to see you, son," she whispers, pressing a kiss to my cheek. I put my arms around her, trying to keep it together as I look down and see my daughter staring up at me, green eyes shining.

"I have cars," she tells me with confidence, lifting up a red Volkswagen Beetle for my inspection. I pull away from my mother and bend down, reaching out a hand to take the toy from her small fingers. "I have fifteen cars," she adds, dropping her hands to her sides and looking up at Lola.

"Hey there, squirt," Lola says, reaching out a hand and placing it atop Lydia's red curls. For a second there, I feel like everything's going to work out. Shoulda known better, right? If it's not one thing, it's another.

DOLL FACE

"Good to see ya again."

"Hello there," my mom says, looking down at Lydia with a protective gleam in her eye that I'm not sure I like. It reminds me of the one she used to get when she felt someone was bullying me or being unfair. A *motherly* sort of gleam. I want my mom to play grandma, not take over my duties entirely. I have a feeling she's going to fucking freak when I tell her I want to take Lydia. I bite my lower lip and hand Lydia her car. "I don't believe we've met?" I don't like the implication in her question, like Lola's *just another girl*. My mom might be aware of my philandering ways, but the only woman she's ever met via yours truly was Asuka.

"Mom, this is Lola Saints, my … " I glance over and we exchange a look. I hate titles, hate fucking labeling things. But okay. Shit. I'm a big boy; I can do this fucking shit. "My girlfriend. We actually just bought a place together," I continue, trying to figure out how to explain the fucked up reality of my life. "With the boys, I mean. Us and the boys."

"You're all … living together?" my dad asks, confused. He's never been one to have many male friends. He doesn't understand the brotherhood I share with Turner, Trey, and Jesse, and for that, at least, I feel sorry for him. I guess if I really think about it, there's at least one aspect of his life that he didn't get perfect. My mom takes my statement in a completely different light.

"You're *staying*?" she whispers, and I nod, rising to my feet and debating the pros and cons of pulling Lydia into a hug. She hasn't called me dad yet, so maybe she doesn't remember my loser ass. Gonna have to change that. It's not too late. She's only three for fuck's sake. God, I could really use a cigarette. "Here? In California?" I force a smile to my face and try to pretend I don't notice my father scanning my tattoos with a critical eye. He's not a big fan of ink, let's just leave it at that.

"Even better than that. Over in Beverly Hills. It's a … well, I guess the only word would be *mansion*. Turner's idea," I add and my mother's face lights up like a fucking Christmas tree. She smoothes her hands down her cream colored blouse.

"Now that *is* good news," she says, turning her smile on Lola. "Not just for us, but for Lydia, too." I cough into my fist and try to figure out the best way to put this.

"Actually, that's kind of what I'm here about." Both my parents frown and Lola reaches out a hand for Lydia.

"Hey doll, want to show me the rest of your cars?" Lydia looks between Lola and my parents for a moment before taking her hand and letting her lead her away from us, proclaiming in a bold voice that she's not three, that she's five years old. I feel a real smile hit me for a moment before my parents' expressions manage to strip that away.

"What are you talking about, Ronald?" my mother asks, and I cringe at the sharpness in her voice. I keep my eyes wide open and focused, try to be the man I want to be, not the man I was. But Goddamn, this is hard. *Asuka, I miss your face like fucking crazy.* I lick my lips and try not to picture her almond shaped eyes and her long, dark hair. *Daisuki,* she'd whisper in my ear as we made love. I love you, in Japanese. I take a deep breath.

"I mean, since I'm putting down roots here, I want Lydia to come and live with me."

My father's laugher hurts ten times more than a scream. I watch him shake his head, and purse my lips into a thin line. My fingers curl at my sides, and even though it'd be totally fucking inappropriate to rip off my shirt and beat the shit out of my old man, I kind of wish that I could. That laugh shows just how far I've fallen in his eyes and it fucking kills me.

"You want your three year old daughter, whom you've just met, to come and live with you and your new girlfriend at some Beverly Hills mansion you bought with your rock star buddies? You're a smart man, Ronnie, try to act like one. Do you have any idea how ridiculous that sounds?"

"She's my daughter," I state coldly, not liking the sudden turn of this meeting. I wanted to get out of the mansion, come see my old fucking room, have a moment of Goddamn normalcy. I should've waited to bring this shit up. "So, yeah, maybe my life is weird, but that doesn't mean I can't be a good father. I'm clean and I've got the time and money to take care of her, so that's what I'm going to do."

"No, what you're going to do is leave her here with us," my dad says while my mom folds her arms across her chest and looks between us like she can't even believe this conversation is happening. "When – *if* – we feel like you've got your life together, then we can talk about transitioning Lydia to life with you. We can start with one or two days a week and go from there. Right now, it's not happening. Son, do you think I didn't see that fiasco of a concert on TV? *That's* the environment you want to raise your child in? Maybe it's time for you to take the money and run. This whole 'rock star'," he makes quotes with his fingers, "life hasn't exactly been kind to you. I mean, just look at the last decade of your life."

"The last decade of my life is a blur but not because of music or even drugs or sex or what the fuck ever," my mom cringes at the word, "but because I lost my *fucking* soul mate in a horrific car accident. Three years after that, I lost my *brother*." I flick a finger against the side of my head and try not to scream. I've been hanging around Turner too long. He wouldn't just scream right now, he'd rage and throw shit and he'd get his way, no matter what. So why the fuck do I feel like I'm about to lose?

"You were eighteen years old, Ronnie. I understand that you loved Asuka, that you were hurting, but you can hardly blame all the mistakes you've made on that one incident. Travis … he was a good boy, but he *wasn't* your brother. A good friend, yes. A nice person, I don't doubt that. Ronnie, you need to take responsibility for your own actions. I love you, and you know that, but I can't in good conscious hand this little girl over to you."

"It's not like you have a choice," I whisper, and I hate how cold my voice sounds, how empty. "You gonna take me to court?"

"If that's what it takes. I know in your mind, it seems like a clear win, but when I present evidence of your drug use, of our involvement in Lydia's life and your lack thereof, maybe things will take a different turn? If you want to go through that, put Lydia through that, so be it."

I clench my teeth and put a hand to my face. *Really* wish I could channel some Turner right now, throw a raging fucking fit. Anyway, what's stopping me from picking Lydia up and walking out of here? My parents wouldn't put up a physical fight, but then again, I don't doubt my father's words. If he thinks he can win in court against me, I should be scared. Fuck, I don't know crap about custody and all that shit. I'm just a fucking drummer. I can slam out a beat that will knock your skull in half, make you beg me to stir up that gray matter between your ears. But court shit? Legal stuff? Uh, fuck that.

"Look, I know I haven't given you guys much reason to trust me, but things are going to be different this time. Sure, my living situation's a little unorthodox, but when are you guys going to figure out that strange doesn't always mean inferior? Sometimes, weird shit's the best." I can tell from my parents' faces that they're not buying what I'm selling. I close my eyes and take a deep breath, taste the sweet scent of sugar in the air. Knowing my mom, she's probably got something in the oven. I always thought that if she weren't so obsessed with being a mother and a housewife, that she might've enjoyed

DOLL FACE

running a bakery or some shit. My mom can bake an apple pie like nobody's business. "Besides, I'm planning on working out a plan to get Phoebe – "

My father's snort of disbelief explodes from his lips before he turns away and looks down at the floor with a sigh, planting his hands on his hips and shaking his head. Fuck.

"Dad." I say the word firmly, looking past my mom and focusing hard on his back. I force my fingers to relax, make myself take long, slow breaths. After a moment, I glance over my shoulder and find Lola seated on the floor with Lydia, her dark hair swinging in her face as she smiles, as she takes a little metal truck from my daughter's hand and runs it up Lydia's arm. Lydia giggles, and I feel my own lips twitch. See. This is the kind of stuff I'm missing out on, the little everyday shit. I know it seems a little hypocritical of me to come bursting in here after three years, but when the clouds clear and you can finally glimpse a bit of sunshine in your life, you don't sit in the fucking dark with the blinds drawn. "Lydia is *my* daughter. I get that I'm in a transitional period, but as soon as I set up a bedroom for her, as soon as I feel like things have settled down a little, I'm taking her with me. For now, expect me here visiting five times a week or more." I turn away and don't bring up Phoebe again. Maybe my parents know something I don't, or maybe they just don't trust me with an infant, I don't care.

I know what I want and what I need at this point in my life and *nobody* – a gun toting psychopath, a needle filled with liquid courage, my parents – is going to stop me from taking it.

CHAPTER 9
& LOLA SAINTS &

Five days and absolutely zero fucks later, I'm so desperate for a naughty that I'm practically salivating, sitting here next to the pool and watching Ronnie as he swims laps. I don't think he's noticed that I'm here yet, but that's fucking fine with me. I'm more than happy to sit 'ere and watch his muscles ripple as he parts the water with strong strokes, propelling that perfect form of his through the water. His ink looks twice as bright submerged beneath the perfect blue surface, and I find myself sucking in a breath that I forget to let out until I get so lightheaded that I start to sway.

"You alright?" Sydney Charell asks, pausing next to

me, a cuppa clutched in her hands and a sleepy look on her face that's at odds with the tightness around her eyes. As soon as Ronnie and I got back from that awkward little encounter with his parents, Sydney was standing in the living room having a screaming argument with her younger brother. After an epic fucking row, she stormed up the stairs and hasn't left since. I guess for now, she's living here, too. Just one big happy Goddamn family. Ah, the bloody irony.

I blow a puff of smoke out and do what I've been doing for days – forcing my mind away from the overwhelming wash of pain that comes whenever I think of my sister. It's been so bad that I haven't even gotten up the courage to call my father, to tell him, or to see if he knows. I mean, shit, he must, right? Nobody's asked me about the funeral. My throat gets tight and I take another drag on my durry.

"Just peachy, babe," I tell her, snuffing the cherry out in a nearby ashtray and closing my eyes as a warm breeze breaks across my skin. I'm still torn between loving it here and being miserable. It's nice to be off the tour, away from Ice and Glass, away from Stephen, but somehow, I feel like we got off too easy. If I was a betting woman, I'd say this wasn't over yet. Not by a long shot.

DOLL FACE

"I'd stay out of the kitchen if I were you," she tells me as Ronnie breaks the surface of the pool and folds his arms on the edge, smiling at me with dark hair dripping into his face. I smile back and my heart skips a few beats. My cunt, not so much. She hits every beat, letting the desperation I feel downstairs hit me up top. My nipples get hard as rocks and I find myself crossing my arms over my chest to hide the reaction from Sydney. The fingers of my left hand and trail down and probe gently at my wound. I'm feeling a fuck of a lot better. Now, if I could only convince Ronnie of that. "Turner just got off the phone with the hospital. No change in Naomi's condition and nobody seems to know exactly *why* she's not waking up." Sydney sighs and closes her eyes, getting out a cigarette of her own as she stands oblivious in her pink bikini. Tattoos stand at sharp attention from her arms, her chest, her sides. I think about what she said, about having a photo shoot sometime soon. I hope our shit doesn't derail hers.

"Gotcha," I say, looking back at Ronnie as he climbs from the pool in his tight ass little budgie smugglers. They're so fucking small that they emphasize exactly how big he really is. My breath hitches and I have to force myself to look away. Sydney's staring off into the distance, eyes cloudy, arms hanging by her side. I want to say something to her, like how happy I am that she's here, but I'm not sure how to go about it. I need a friend right now, am fucking desperate for it. My subconscious whispers evil things, tellin' me I'm trying to replace Poppet with somebody else's sister.

I light up another cigarette as Ronnie moves across the pavement towards me, leaving wet footprints in his wake. The smell of chlorine mixes with the spicy sweetness of the tobacco, and I sigh.

"Morning, babe," he says, leaning down and pressing his lips against mine. The gesture's so familiar, so personal and casual, I'm not really sure how to respond. My mouth, though, she's not suffering from the same mental hang-ups. I find my hand drawn to the back of Ronnie's wet head, my tongue diving into his mouth as a thrill of heat washes over me and I shudder. He feels it, I know he does, but whether he's refusing to acknowledge it because of my injury or because of the shit week he's having, I'm not sure. Phoebe's parents won't answer the phone and visits with Lydia are still stiff and uncomfortable. I had hoped meeting my new bloke's mum and dad would go over a bit better than this, but they hardly look at me. There's so much baggage between Ronnie and them that even though I can tell they love each other, they refuse to work past it. It's

DOLL FACE

frustratingly as all fuck out. Or maybe I'm just horny? "Got any plans today?"

"Same as yesterday and the day before that. Same as tomorrow and a week from now. Nope, nope, and nope." I smoke my cigarette as Ronnie stands up and nods at Sydney. "Why?" I look up at him as he grabs a towel from a nearby chair and wraps it around his hips, hiding that perfectly pleasant bulge between his legs from sight. *Damn.* "You do?"

Ronnie coughs into his hand and glances away, towards the outdoor barbeque area that none of us have used yet. That sort of thing's reserved for celebrations, and nobody in this friggin' house is in the mood to celebrate. Too many dead people, too much fucked up shit. I sigh and a cloud of gray smoke wafts in the air for just a moment, clinging to an oncoming breeze and whispering away through the palm trees. In the distance, I can hear a slight murmur of voices. There's a crowd out front, you bet your ass there is. Started off about two days after we moved in. I like to think it looks smaller, but that just might be my dying optimism having a go at me, the bitch.

"I got to get Turner out of the house for a while," he begins, and I tilt my head to the side, trying not to focus too hard on that lily tattoo of his. If I do, I'm liable to cream my fucking panties. *I'm so sex deprived! It's not fair.* Not only am I a red-blooded woman with needs, but since I'm trying my best to lay off the good stuff – the drugs and the alcohol – I need *something* to keep my mind off the toilet that is my life. I try to tell myself that I'm livin' it up with a rock star, kicking the shit in a mansion with no responsibilities, but the reality's a lot less pretty than all of that. I'm a girl with no future, no band, no money, no visa. I'm afraid that if I blink, I'll find myself back to being a cane cocky's daughter, picking up the dead mice that the cats always leave lying around the barn. "Anyway," Ronnie continues, drawing me out of my thoughts. "I need to get Turner out and about and … " He gives Sydney a look and she smiles, holding up her hands and backing away without a word. I thought privacy would be hard to come by, living in a house with all these people, but it almost feels like the opposite. I'm almost … lonely. "So we're going to get tested."

I raise an eyebrow.

"Tested," I repeat, thinking of Ronnie, handing me a condom for a blow job. If he's *that* worried about it, I guess I should be glad. Instead, I just feel empty. I don't want to feel like this anymore. I want that life, that excitement back that we had at the beginning of the tour.

DOLL FACE

Sure, I'm glad I'm not working for Stephen anymore, but I need *something*. Life. I need to see the wheels turning and the cart rolling along towards greener pastures. I'm just not sure how to make that happen. "Sounds like a bloody brilliant way to spend a day."

Ronnie chuckles and reaches out a finger, drawing the whorl of his fingertip against my lips. I sigh and lean into the touch, my cigarette held out at my side, my chest heaving with desperation. Transition. Nobody ever told me it was a dirty word, but it is, and it's hard, and it *sucks*.

"Let me know the results as soon as you get 'em," I say, pushing his hand away and rising to my feet. I look up at Ronnie's face because to look at his chest or his abs or his tattoos would be too much right now, and I make myself smile. "If you're clean, I wouldn't mind a bit of raw doggin', if you catch my drift." His laughter follows me as I turn and head back inside, finding Sydney sitting in her bikini in the kitchen. Her breasts sit on the edge of the counter, propped up by the granite like they're too heavy to stay up on their own. Only I know that's not true. Sydney's fake ass tits are nice. I won't say I'm jealous, but they look good on her.

"Any word from Dax?" I ask, wishing for someone else's drama to come in and save me from myself. I open the fridge door, marveling at the expansive mass of stainless steel and step back, surveying the contents within. Since we can't easily go out right now, Milo ordered in groceries. There's more than enough leafy greens in here to last me a lifetime: tomatoes, peppers, cucumbers, and in the cabinet last night I found chia seeds and whole grain bread. Nothing I much feel like eating. I want some fucking takeaway, like a Mrs. Mac's Pie from the service station. My stomach rumbles and I press a hand over it.

"He's ... staying at a hotel downtown. The same one you guys stayed at actually. I've only seen him once since the concert, and he doesn't look good. I know he'd hate to hear me say this, but he's a sensitive guy. He doesn't deserve all of this shit." I hear a slamming sound and turn to find Sydney closing her magazine with more force than necessary, sitting up and staring at me from a pretty face surrounded by perfect blonde hair. Colorful sea creatures crawl across her neck and chest, her shoulders, her arms. I like 'em. Makes her seem more animated somehow, more alive. Don't understand anyone who doesn't have ink. "I want to see him again, but I don't know how to go about doing it. If I call, he answers, but what can I say? Me and him, we're nothing to each other." Sydney sighs and purses her lips, blue

DOLL FACE

eyes sparkling with *something*. I'm not sure what – anger, frustration, longing – but I can at tell that at the very least, she wishes they weren't nothing.

After staring longingly at the raw contents of the fridge, I close it, wishing they'd morph into something edible. My stomach rumbles again, and Sydney smiles.

"Think we could get a pizza delivered here?" she asks, and I shrug. I don't know shit about shit when it comes to 'celebrity' life. Pretty sure that's what Indecency qualifies as now. Can't turn on the fucking TV without seeing their faces, can't read a magazine without seeing an article, can't go online without finding them trending somewhere or other. This morning on Twitter, all I saw was #turnermotherfuckingcampbell, #indecency, #amatoryriot, #naomiknox, and #rocknroll. Pretty clear that the public mind is still firmly entrenched in our shit.

I reach across the kitchen island and snag an apple from the silver bowl there, biting into it and wondering if Milo Terrabotti intends on living here with his band. I'm not sure if I've seen him leave once since we got here. To be honest, I feel sorry for the man; he works his fucking ass off taking care of these boys.

"We could always call and tell 'em to bring our shit to the biggest, most ostentatious house on the block," I suggest, leaning against the counter and closing my eyes against this brief slice of normalcy. I might be standing in a kitchen worth more than my family's entire farmhouse, but this feels real. I *need* real right now.

I open my eyes and watch Sydney reach out for her cell, sliding her fingers across the screen as I munch on my apple and wrinkle my brow. My body's itching for music. I want to hit a kit, slam my sticks and feel a beat work its way under my skin. If Ronnie happens to be standing behind me while I play, sliding his fingers along my inner thigh, reaching up to that sweet, hot space under my skirt … *fuck.* I bite my lip and shake my head, putting my fingers against my temple. One track mind, anybody?

"Yeah, that's great," Sydney's saying, giving me a thumbs-up. I smile back at her and drop my hand, finishing off my apple and looking around for a rubbish bin. She gets up, still on the phone and smiles, kicking at a spot on the lower cabinets. A drawer pops out and voila, there it is in all its fantastical stainless steel glory. "Trash compactor," she mouths as she pulls on the handle and opens it for me. "See you in forty," Sydney finishes, hanging up her phone and giving me a raised eyebrow as I shake my head in disbelief.

"Whatever happened to a simple, plastic bin?" I ask,

finding the situation suddenly funny. "Or, like when I was growing up, a freaking bucket? We'd just toss our rubbish in there and my dad would take it out and light it on fucking fire." I poke the stainless steel with my foot and throw up my arms, tilting my head back and taking a deep breath. Shit, I don't want anyone to think I'm complaining about all this luxury. It's just … not me.

"Consider yourself lucky that you *had* a garbage can and a dad that gave a shit. My dad was always coked up and trying to figure out what his next scheme was going to be, you know, to get more money to buy more fucking crack." Sydney laughs and leans against the counter like she actually finds her story amusing. I search her eyes for pain, and can only find the slightest sliver of pity. She's over her childhood, really over it. I'm impressed. "Anyway," Sydney waves her hand and forges on with her story, "he used to just throw garbage, let it lie where it may, you know? So Trey and I, of course, followed in his footsteps. I think I was seven or eight before I realized it wasn't normal to walk around in a foot of smelly crap." Sydney sighs and shakes her head, pointing down at the trash compactor. "So as ridiculously stupid as this thing is, I kind of like it."

"Kind of like what?" her brother asks, wheeling himself into the kitchen and around the center island.

Trey looks like shit still, making me feel like a complete horse's ass again. Seems kind of fucked that we'd both get shot, but that I'd walk away from it easy while he's stuck in that chair, suffering. The universe works in mysterious ways – most of them pretty fucked up. I try to smile at Trey and he returns the look with a wary one, like he doesn't trust me. Rightfully so, I guess. I have no idea what Ronnie's told him about me, but I hope this works out. I really do. The fact that these people are even still talking to me is a miracle – let alone letting me live in their house. I cross my arms over my chest and try to breathe. "What is that anyway?"

Sydney snorts and ruffles her brother's brown hair.

"It's called a trash compactor, dumb ass. You put garbage in and then you press a button and it smashes it all together." She claps her hands and her tits jiggle like nobody's business. Trey notices and wrinkles his nose. "You don't have to take it out as often, makes life easier." She shrugs and Trey scowls, like a Turner clone.

"Who cares about that? Milo says he's hiring a cleaning staff anyway." Trey rolls himself back a few feet and angles towards the fridge, reaching out to pull it open while his sister looks on in disgust.

"Cleaning staff or not, that doesn't mean you can just

DOLL FACE

throw your shit on the ground. I hope you're aware of that." Trey ignores her and Sydney sighs again, waving her hand dismissively and pushing off from the counter. "After the pizza gets here," she says and then glances over at her brother, "and you're paying by the way," he snorts but doesn't offer up a smart ass comment, "I was thinking of going to the hospital to visit Naomi." Sydney pauses and glances away for a moment before turning her blue eyes back to mine. "Blair's there, too, and she's not doing well at all. I thought maybe Dax might show up … "

Sydney trails off, and I smile.

"I'll be there," I say, because if I'm going to make a life of it here, I'm going to need friends. Sydney seems like as good a place to start as any.

✗ ✗ ✗

Naomi Knox looks beautiful, like a sleeping princess or some shit. If I believed in all of that fairy-tale crap, I'd be calling up Turner and asking him to stop by and give her a deep, sexy pash to wake her arse up. I cross my arms over my chest and lean back, looking down at the spread of blonde hair around her face, at Sydney as she combs out the tangles. In the fucking movies, people in comas always have perfect hair, don't they? But Naomi's was a rat's nest before we got to it. She still looks pretty though, like a fucking rock star.

"What happens if she never wakes up?" I ask, feeling yet another stab of guilt through the gut. *God.* I can't help but taste the impact of my involvement in all of this, like a blob of rotten fruit, molding and turning to mush on the tip of my tongue. No matter how hard I try, I can't wash away the fucking guilt. "What happens to Turner?"

Sydney takes a step back and slaps the wooden brush against the palm of her hand. She's switched out her pink bikini for a black tank and some skinny jeans, a pair of red suede boots and an armful of those rubber bracelets everyone's always picking up at the concerts. Most of my shit's missing – all I've got right now is a single duffel bag, one that I took to the concert with me. It had exactly two of my comfiest dresses in it, a pair of jeans, a few pairs of panties, and a bra. Ronnie asked Milo about the clothing situation and some chick, some 'personal shopper' or whatever the fuck you want to call 'er, brought back a couple of bags of stuff for me.

DOLL FACE

Surprisingly, the clothes were dead on with my style, but they still don't feel right. Oh, you know, like I've got a fucking bullet wound on my belly, so my usual look doesn't really work right now. I settled for wearing a new leather jacket and one of the many, many band T-shirts that float around us like clouds. Swear to Christ, I could reach around blind in anybody's bag with my eyes closed and come up with another of the bloody things. Today's tee is navy blue with *Terre Haute'*s logo on the front.

"If Naomi never wakes up … I imagine Turner will transform into some fucked up clone of Ronnie." Sydney cringes and glances quickly over her shoulder at me. I focus on her orange octopus tattoo instead of her eyes. I know the pain Ronnie went through, or at least a fraction of it. I can feel Poppet's loss like a knife through the heart, twisting in my chest with every breath. I just force myself not to think about it. My fingers twitch and unconsciously, I find myself reaching for my jacket pocket, digging in and feeling a wash of disappointment when I don't come in contact with one of the little plastic vodka bottles I'm so used to carrying around. "I mean, old Ronnie, of course. You have no idea the change you've made in him."

Sydney turns back to Naomi and lays a hand across her forehead.

C.M. STUNICH

"But she'll wake up. I know she will. I can feel it."

I nod, but I don't say anything. Sydney told me on the way over here, in the back of one of those swanky security vans, that she felt like an outsider. Only, she's not the real outsider here. *I* am. Sydney's known these boys all their lives; I've only just met them. I'm hanging onto this group by a thin thread, wrapped around Ronnie's pinky finger and liable to snap at any moment. *Don't think about the marriage thing,* I tell myself. And then of course, I do. *Shit.* Ronnie didn't drop to his knees or anything, but he definitely suggested it. The thought's one part terrifying, two parts exhilarating. I'm not sure what to think about that.

"Ready to pay Blair a visit?" she asks and I shrug. I don't know the girl, but if there's a chance Dax could be there, I should go for Sydney's sake. Hey, who wouldn't jump at another chance to have guilt rammed down their throat like a dry dildo? Here's to the show of hands. Sydney slides her fingers across Naomi's forehead and turns toward the door, moving past the security guard with us like he's not even there. She insisted we didn't need one, but I'm starting to learn that when Milo Terrabotti wants something, he can be fairly convincing.

"When's your photo shoot?" I ask, thinking of *Tattoo Terror,* the website Cohen used to beat off to. He'd leer at

DOLL FACE

me whenever I walked in on him, dick in hand, and flash me the screen. *I have to use these bitches to get off because you're not good enough.* I shiver and cut off that train of thought. Last thing I need today is a trip down memory lane, one that only leads to an impossible puzzle where I try to figure out how Cohen changed from a sweetheart to an asshole in an instant.

"It *was* going to be in a few days," Sydney whispers, her voice cracking as we move down the hall, fluorescent lighting cutting into my eyeballs and giving me a migraine. She seems to know where she's going, so I keep pace and ignore the stretching and tugging of the skin around my wound. It seems to be healing up nicely, but I can feel it with every step I take. "But, after all the publicity surrounding the concert and whatnot, I got a call that the shoot's been temporarily canceled." I wrinkle my brows.

"Canceled? Bloody fuck. What the hell does that mean?" Sydney keeps her gaze straight ahead and doesn't look at me.

"I don't know. You'd think me being the sister of Indecency's lead guitarist would help with their subscribers, boost advertising revenue, I don't know, *something*. But my guess? They just don't want any of that poison around their magazine." Sydney sighs and runs a hand through her perfect blonde hair. Her bangs are cut so sharp, framing her eyes with a perfectly straight line of white blonde. It gives her an edgy look that I'm sure would bring douche bags like Cohen swarming to the company's website.

"Well, I'll be stuffed," I snort, shaking my head. "The rotten reaching arm of this shit extends to all facets of life, doesn't it? I wonder if America and Stephen knew that would happen when they started their war, or if they even cared."

"What I want to know is who did what exactly. Everything that happened – Ronnie's kids being dumped with their mothers' bodies, Dax's mom being shipped in the back of a van to the hotel, the sniper that got Trey – how much of that was Stephen and how much was America?" Sydney looks over at me, her eyes like the waters that drown The Great Barrier Reef. Bright, open, honest. Fuck those fuckers at *Tattoo Terror;* they're missing out. "I mean, how much do you know exactly?" she asks, and I cringe.

"Not a whole lot to be honest with you. Everybody in Ice and Glass had their targets and that was that. I was supposed to make Ronnie fall in love with me or some stupid shit like that, traumatize the poor fuck and take him down so deep he'd never climb out. There were bets

DOLL FACE

in the band on whether I could get him to commit suicide or not." I feel my heart twist in my chest. When Stephen lured us in, it was with vague hints that we'd have to pay a price for his patronage, that he'd make us stars, that our music would be immortalized. When he started giving us tasks, I thought they were weird, but manageable. Send a doll head to Naomi Knox, a baseball cap to Indecency's bus. Sneak this guy, this Eric Rhineback, behind the scenes. I could do all that. When things first started to take a turn for the worse, I didn't know what to do and neither did anybody else. When it came time to put on those masks, storm that bus … we just did as we were told. My stomach flip flops and I cover my mouth with my hand.

"Sorry," Sydney says as she pauses outside of a hospital room door. Instead of a police officer, there's one of Brayden's guards standing outside the room, just like at Naomi's. I didn't even bother to ask the guy what his fucking deal was. What's the point? Obviously Brayden's not quite done with us yet. I guess he's got to stick around and make sure Naomi and Blair get their stories straight. "I didn't mean to bring it up." Sydney takes a deep breath and gives me a tight-lipped smile before knocking on the door. The guard pays us no attention.

A moment later, the door opens and Dax appears, face full of stubble, dark hair greasy and unwashed, lips downturned at the corners. When he sees us standing there, he sighs like he's relieved and leans against the door like he can barely carry his own body weight.

"Hey," he whispers and I watch as Sydney visibly holds herself back. She wants to touch him, to put her arms around his neck and tell him that everything's going to be okay. Instead, she twists her hands together, the full sleeves of her tattoos a colorful swirl of nervousness.

"How is she?" Sydney asks, peering around Dax's shoulder at the comatose form on the bed. He takes a step back and ushers us inside before closing the door behind us. There's a chair sitting next to the bed, covered with a rumpled blanket and a white pillow. On the table next to it, there's a vase of flowers and a tray of untouched food. The entire room reeks of despair and misery. Poor fucker.

"Not much better," he grumbles, sinking into the chair and straightening the wrinkled purple T-shirt he's wearing. "She was shot twice in the chest." Dax makes a gun with his hand and points it at his pecs, pretending to pull the trigger. "Each bullet managed to find a lung, so Blair was basically suffocating while we waited for an ambulance." He stares at his friend for a long moment

DOLL FACE

and then looks away. Sydney and I both take a step closer to the bed and look down at the keyboardist's expression. I know she's a beautiful girl, but right now, she's got a face like a dropped pie. It's all squinched up and pale, her lips bloodless, her hair tangled and ratty.

Sydney doesn't say anything, just exchanges a glance with me over her body and then starts to comb the black and blonde hair into place. This could be a sign that Naomi might come out of her coma soon. If she looks that good and poor Blair here looks that bad ... I glance up at Dax as he continues to talk.

"Her mom told me the doctor said there's a good chance she'll have permanent brain damage." He swallows and tucks his legs up on the chair, wrapping his arms around them and resting his chin on his knees. Dax McCann is not in a good place right now. "Her family's been staying here ever since they flew in, but I made 'em take a break. They went back to the hotel to rest for a little while." He sighs and lets his gray eyes close enough that I can read the words on the back of the lids. *Born Wrong.*

"I'm so sorry," I say, but he doesn't open his eyes or look at me. Maybe he blames me for this, maybe not, but that room suddenly feels so small and stifling that I feel like I've got to get out of there. The walls start to close in and my breath comes in shallow bursts. As if it can sense my anxiety, my bullet wound begins to throb. "I'm going to … take an early mark," I say and get a funny look from Sydney. Whether that's because of my slang or because I'm acting like a cracked out lunatic, I'm not sure. I can feel little beads of sweat dripping down my forehead as I back away and turn towards the door. "I'll be in the hallway if you need me." I step out and close it behind me, still panting, drawing a strange look from the guard to my right. Fuck him.

I stumble down the hall a bit and collapse into a row of blue plastic chairs. The leopard print ballet flats on my feet look garish against the white glimmer of the linoleum floor. I close my eyes and let my fingers curl around the seat of the chair while I struggle against the rush of emotions that I know I can't keep pushing back forever.

Blair's just another innocent bystander in a war that had nothing to do with me, with her, with Ronnie. I shouldn't ever have gotten involved. Just being around Dax for an instant, feeling his pain, thinking about Hayden and Katie and all the other people who lost their lives because of it, makes me feel like I *deserved* to lose Poppet. Maybe that was my punishment for all the things I was involved in, all of the crap I let slide.

DOLL FACE

I feel tears threatening to push out from under my eyelids, and I fight them back with everything I've got. I won't sit here and do this, not right now. I open my eyes again and stare at a pair of stainless steel water fountains across the hall from me. Nurses and doctors stream past and nobody pays me any attention until Dina, the bitch nurse from hell walks by. As soon as she catches sight of me, she pauses.

"Miss Saints." Her voice scrapes across my raw nerves like a cheese grater over cheddar. I wrinkle my mouth and raise my gaze up to meet hers. "How are you feeling?" She pauses in front of me, red hair slicked back on her head like a ballet dancer. There's a bun sitting on top of her skull, dead center, a red lump that gives the woman a strong resemblance to one of those creepy cartoon characters in *How the Grinch Stole Christmas!*.

I shrug and Dina's already frowning mouth seems to sink deeper into her face.

"Don't forget your follow up visits," she reminds me, but I'm sure I probably will anyway. I lean back and rest my arms on the backs of the chairs on either side of me. We continue to stare at one another until I get so miffed at having my personal space invaded that I decide to see if I can piss her off, just to get her to go away.

"Nick off, you rat bag," I mumble as she digs her feet in and seems determined to bother me. Her green gaze seems familiar somehow, or maybe I'm just imagining that, comparing the mossy color of her eyes to my memory of Brayden Ryker's. Weird ass motherfucker. I still don't get how he plays into all of this. Since he seems to suck some serious dick when it comes to actually providing security for the people he's supposed to be protecting, there must be some other angle he's playing, something I'm not getting. The fact that I'm just as far away from the truth now as I was on the night of the concert bugs me.

"Pushing me away won't do you any good. I'm only trying to help." I roll my eyes, but nothing can make me forget the way she jabbed needles into my arm, with that extra special little bit of unnecessary force. "Just because you're hurting on the inside doesn't mean you need to project that pain onto others. It's not fair, and it's not acceptable. Rudeness should never be tolerated from anyone." She pauses here. "Not even from a 'rock star'." The little quotes she makes with her fingers give me a raging headache.

"Pull ya head in. You don't know what you're talking about. Piss off, mate." I let my eyes drift down the hall, towards Blair's door. There's no sign of Sydney or Dax

DOLL FACE

yet, so I turn my attention back to Dina. If she thinks she can bully me out of here, she's dead wrong. I can be a real stubborn bitch when needed.

"Well, I just thought you should know that your boyfriend's downstairs and on his way up." I raise my right eyebrow.

"Ronnie?"

"No," Dina says with an annoying half-smile. "Cohen Rose. As soon as you checked in as a visitor, I let him know you were here. I'm sure he'll be *thrilled* to see you." My blood chills as Nurse Dina moves away with a squeak of white sneakers against the polished linoleum. My nostrils flare and the scent of iodine becomes so overwhelming that I almost puke, right there on the perfectly perfect hospital floor. My head spins and I lean over, struggling to take in a deep breath.

"Hey there, Lola." I hear Cohen's voice before I see him, keeping my gaze focused on my feet until I feel like I can look up without getting sick. Several pairs of footsteps approach, and I raise my chin to look over at Cohen, standing shakily next to me with a pale face and disheveled hair. Looking at him now, I find it hard to believe I ever let him get the best of me. As soon as he started beating me, I should've knocked his ass out. Only

I didn't. Just like with my bitch of a mum, I let him hit me and I didn't do a damn thing about it, not for a long, long time. I guess even before I was a murderer and a traitor, I felt like I deserved to be punished.

I spare a quick glance for the men on either side of Cohen. Brown hair, plain faces, muscular chests. Brayden Ryker's men. Again. Hmm.

"What do you want, Cohen?" I ask, enjoying the twinge of venom in my words. At least I can still manage that. His shit brown eyes bore into me as he shifts and adjusts his right arm, trapped in a sling by his side. If that was my doing, I'm not sure. When I took that second shot at Cohen, I have no idea if I even hit gold. I hope so. I try to take pleasure in that. "Don't you have a plane to catch back to Arkansas or something? There must be a trailer park out there with your name written all over it."

"Listen to me, you little bitch," he growls and then pauses when Brayden's men shift next to him. This whole operation here stinks of subterfuge and underground politics. I don't like it. Scares the shit out of me. Blackness creeps in at the edges of my vision, and I start to wonder if our whole *it's all over now* motto might be a little premature. It doesn't *feel* over. No, the shit storm still seems to be raging, even if all the diarrhea is falling behind the scenes. "Listen to me, Lola.

DOLL FACE

Whatever you think, whatever that Ronnie guy's made you believe, it's all a load of bullshit. This isn't over, so don't go riding off into the sunset just yet. I was promised my piece, and it hasn't been delivered. Joel is ... " Another uncomfortable shift from Brayden's men. "Dead. Honesty and Chris are damn close to it. We were *promised* fame. And money. I don't see any of that shit happening."

"Oh, get stuffed, Cohen. I don't have time to sit here and listen to your maniacal cackling." I shake my head and force my hands to sit still in my lap. I won't give this asshole the pleasure of seeing me squirm. His crap brown eyes are searching right now, gleefully seeking weakness to feed off of. That's his thing, you know. He's an insecure man looking for more, more, more. It's bloody terrifying. "I don't know why you're not sitting in jail somewhere. Hell, I don't know why *I'm* not sitting in jail somewhere." I feel Brayden's guards looking very closely at me, so I keep it vague. "But what I do know is that it looks like I'm going to get a second chance. Sorry to burst your bubble, but if I can walk away from all of this and take it, I damn well will. Make your own destiny, Cohen, and stop relying on others to do it for you." I smile and it feels like the expression is eating away at my face. "Your dick's not big enough to entice anyone to stay for the sex and you've got a few roos loose in the top paddock. If I could pass on any advice at this point, it would be to stop beating your girlfriends and act like a gentleman for a change."

Cohen's hands curl into fists by his sides and his nostrils flare, but he doesn't take another step towards me. Instead he scrubs a hand through his dirty blonde hair and scowls.

"You can't be redeemed. You know that, right? A bitch that's done all the things you've done? Whatever fantasyland you're living in, you might want to dig yourself out and take a look around you. Just because Stephen's dead doesn't mean you're free to do as you please." Cohen licks his lips and opens his mouth for a second tirade when something he sees behind me stops him in his tracks.

"Do I need to take my fucking shirt off again, Cohen?" Ronnie asks as I sit up suddenly and whip my head around to stare at him through fluttering strands of brunette that settle gently around my face as I stare at the best damn drummer that ever walked this earth. My mouth gets dry and my heartbeat picks up at the sight of him cracking his knuckles and frowning at my ex. Turner stands on his left, a smirk curling up the corners of his lips. The fluorescent lights make the piercing in his

DOLL FACE

tongue gleam when he opens his mouth to speak.

"I hear last time this motherfucker went after you, you pissed yourself. Too bad I wasn't around to see it. Why don't you keep messing with his woman and let's see how far he lets you go before he smashes your face in." Considering Cohen's still sporting some of the bruises that Ronnie left on his face in Wichita, I'm surprised he's got the balls to actually open his fat ass mouth again.

"So I insulted some dead Asian bitch. Big fucking deal." Cohen points at me and lets a smirk move over his mouth, one that he modeled after his idol, Turner Campbell. Thing is, that look on Turner's face is legit. On Cohen's? Eh. Not so much. "And I've gotten my dick wet with this cunt enough times that I feel like I got the right to talk to her however I damn well please." Ronnie takes a few steps forward, but Brayden's men bristle, like they're not about to let any shit go down here. Ah. I see. Cohen doesn't actually have any balls; he's just grandstanding because he thinks having two muscled men at his back makes him immune to getting his ass kicked.

I rise to my feet and give Ronnie a look, taking in his black T-shirt with the red rose, the cursive writing that says *Bloom Big, Bleed Bright*. The cotton fabric stretches across his muscles, reminding me yet again that I haven't been laid in way too fucking long. Closest thing I've had in the last ten or whatever days was that magical bit of tongue in the hotel room. My body makes sure I don't miss Ronnie's well-fitting jeans, the ones that are at least two sizes smaller than he normally wears, but also two sizes bigger than Turner's – at least.

"It's okay, love, I got this," I tell him, putting a hand on his chest and cutting off a rush of hormones that floods my brain and makes me feel a little loopy. "We've had enough violence on this tour." I look back at Cohen with a stern expression. "Cohen Rose was on his way out." I pat Ronnie and take a step back, watching as Turner looks between my ex and Ronnie with one raised brow, wondering if he's going to go for it anyway, Brayden's men be damned.

I move away from the new man in my life and turn back towards Cohen, getting as close to him as the guards will allow before I put a smile on my face and look between them.

"One hug for the road, one last hurrah for the relationship we used to have, the one that wasn't so bad before you turned rogue." I shrug and hold out my arms. Cohen looks confused as fuck, but that's normal. He's definitely not the sharpest knife in the drawer. "No wucking furries," I tell him and he wrinkles his face up

DOLL FACE

like I'm retarded. Too much Aussie slang for the stupid little Yank, I guess. "No fucking worries," I clarify, keeping my arms wide and wiggling my fingers, "I don't bite."

"You know what, screw you, Lola," Cohen says, backing up and proving that sometimes a little nicety goes a long way to pissing somebody off. Only I'm not just trying to scare Cohen away or prove some new world bullshit about how violence never solves anything. I'm trying to clobber the scummy little creep in the face. Just a little closer ... I take a step towards Cohen, arms still open and then sigh, dropping them to my side like I'm done here. "Why don't you go back to the Outback where you belong? Go fuck a koala or some shit. I'm done here." Cohen starts to turn away and I wrap my fingers around his arm. He pauses a moment to look back at me. Big mistake on his part.

A smile steals across my lips, but neither of Brayden's bitches moves in to separate us. I guess with my big eyes and my fun sized little body, nobody thinks of me as much of a threat.

"Deal. I mean, I'd rather fuck a koala than touch your short fat little dick again. Never in my life have I had to ask *is it in* before. Cohen, you should be ashamed of yourself." Before he can tear his arm from my grip, I curl the fingers of my right hand into a fist and let it fly, smashing my knuckles right into Cohen Rose's ugly ass face. The wheedling scream that tears from his throat and the accompanying droplets of blood that splatter the floor are more than worth the rough grasp of Brayden's men as they pull me back and my belly grumbles in pain, the tender skin stretching as they shove me back and I fall into Ronnie's hard body.

Gentle fingers curl around my arms and I can feel a smile beaming against my back as Cohen screams something incoherent at me and then storms off, boots squeaking across the floor. If I never see that man again, it'll be too soon. I pray that I never will, but knowing my luck, he'll probably be waiting on my bed for me when I get home.

Life's always fucked like that, isn't it?

CHAPTER 10
⚜ Ronnie McGuire ⚜

When somebody says *get tested,* the thoughts that come to mind aren't so bad. I mean, I figured maybe I'd piss in a cup, get some blood drawn or whatever, but I had no clue. No fucking clue. Some dude in rubber gloves stuck a freaking swab in my pee hole. Yeah. You heard me. I got a Goddamn Q-tip shoved in my dick. The only positive part of the experience was hearing Turner's roar of rage from the next room. It took me ten minutes to calm him down after that and convince him to go through with the whole thing. But at least now we'll both know. Too bad I couldn't get Jesse to come with us. He just miraculously disappeared about the time we had to go.

Fucking asshole.

"I think we should go somewhere," Sydney says as we stand outside in a circle and smoke cigarettes. The area around the hospital is some sort of stupid fucking 'smoke free zone', so we had to cross the street with all of our fucking bodyguards in tow and sequester ourselves near the faculty apartments. We huddle next to the back wall of one of the buildings like junior high school students trying to find a spot to grab a smoke, terrified one of our teachers is going to come around the corner at any second and bust us all.

The thought makes me chuckle.

"Go somewhere?" Dax coughs and then shakes his head. Looking at him right now makes me sick to my stomach. He's not in a good place. I don't know the guy, but I'm actually pretty fucking worried about him. I tried to bum a cigarette from him, but he gave me a sharp smile and told me he didn't have anything I'd want. Dax isn't just smoking with us; he's getting wet. That little stick in his hand, the one that looks like a motherfucking cigarette? That's actually a dippy. A smoke dipped in angel dust. I always stayed away from that fucking crap, even when I was at my worst. Angel dust will fuck you so hard that you won't remember which end is up. Emptiness, isolation, loneliness. The first and only time I ever tried a dippy, I came *this* close to killing myself. Yes, drugs can numb the pain but having them numb my entire soul to the point of oblivion? No thanks.

But I'm in no place here to tell Dax what to do with his life. It's his body, his heart, his soul.

"Like, to party or something?" Dax asks, giving Sydney a look that's half irritation, half hope. He wants to stay in the hospital, watch over Blair and Naomi, but he's also desperate to get the hell out of there.

"Yeah, I mean," Sydney stands on her toes and peers over Turner's shoulder, "anywhere but here. Get out and do something." We all follow her gaze and freeze when a woman walks by carrying a pair of reusable shopping bags. She gives us a look and wrinkles her nose at the cigarette smoke but doesn't say anything. Either she doesn't watch the news and has no idea who the fuck we are, or she doesn't care. *Thank God.* I pull out my phone again and Google myself – weird, I know – but I can't seem to stop doing it. I'm terrified my STD results are going to end up on the Internet before they land in my hands. I give a passing thought to Paulette Washington and then shake it off. No reality show, no fucking way.

"Isn't that, like, sacrilegious or some shit?" Turner asks, holding his cig in one hand and crossing the other over his belly. His eyes are faraway and his voice sounds hollow. After Lola punched Cohen Rose in the face and turned my cock rock solid with desperation for her, Turner wandered off to start making preparations to take Naomi back to the house. Not sure if that went well or not because he won't talk about it. I slide my gaze to Lola, standing to my right, her body radiating heat that makes my mouth water and my hands shake. This could very well be the longest stretch of my life without sex since I lost my virginity way back when. It *hurts*. Can't say I'm a fan, but I also can't fuck a woman with a gunshot wound. Let's just say, my hand is *exhausted*.

"How so?" Sydney says, sweeping blonde hair away from her face. "We're not dead. We're not zombies. This is life, and it never stops, not even if we want it to. You, Dax, Lola," she gestures around the group, "you all need to get out. We don't have to do anything crazy. Let's just go grab some drinks or something. I think it'd be good for all of us." She finishes her cigarette and crushes it out on the sidewalk with her red suede boots.

"Where are we supposed to go though?" Lola asks, her big bug eyed sunglasses in place, blocking her blue eyes from my gaze. There's a string of tension between us that's stretching tighter and tighter with each passing day. Since the day we officially met, backstage at one of our OKC concerts, we've been fucking like rabbits. The last two weeks? Not so much. "I mean, we'd get mobbed on our way to the dunny. How the hell are we supposed to go clubbing?"

Turner coughs and throws his cigarette down beside Sydney's, eyes still glazed over, voice a lot softer than I'd like to hear it. The overconfident, cocky, asshole attitude is Turner in a good mood. I miss it when he's not throwing insults and flipping everybody off, grabbing his junk and just generally being a prick. *That's* my brother. If you don't like it, fuck off.

"I know a place," he says absently, but not like he really cares. I'm going to have to keep a close eye on him if we go anywhere. I won't let him screw up what he has with Naomi – not that I think he would, but it never hurts to be cautious. "I took Naomi there the night before the concert. It's called Slick's." I take a drag on my cigarette and watch him lift his gaze up, drag a smirk onto his lips that doesn't feel real, like a mask of his usual self. I shiver despite the warmth from above.

"You've tried to drag us there before," I tell him, thinking this must be the club with the secret bathroom entrance.

"You mean I *have* dragged you there before, numb

nuts. You were just too high to remember that shit. We can party there with all the other riffraff that infests this town." Turner sighs and glances at Dax or more specifically, at his dippy. I watch my friend run his tongue across his lower lip as he fights the craving and – thankfully – finds the courage to fight it back for another day. "We'll be safe there. We can drink ourselves into a stupor and dance with people so famous they almost make us look ordinary." Turner tosses a wink at the group and gets out another smoke.

"Tight quarters, lots of people, crazy ass twerking," I say and Lola smiles, "are you sure you're up for that?" She pauses and uses her left hand to pull up her shirt, revealing a patch of bandages. We all watch quietly as she peels them back and reveals what essentially looks like a massive scab. There are dark lines around the edges, stitches. But overall, it doesn't look too bad. I move around behind her and check the exit wound, pulling up the white gauze from Lola's back. Her body shivers as my fingertips graze her spine and my dick springs to life. Sydney sees and rolls her eyes at me. "Well, fuck me. It looks a hell of a lot better than it did a few days ago."

"I'm an Aussie," Lola says, dropping her shirt back into place. She smiles with those full lips of hers, the

DOLL FACE

red-pink of her lipstick bright against her white teeth. "We're made of tough shit. If you guys want to party, I say let's go for it. I'm not sure if I could stand another night in."

"Fucking awesome," Turner says, pulling his cell from his pocket and swallowing hard. Nobody else might notice the gesture, but I do. It's not going to be the same without Naomi. It'll *never* be the same without her. *Jesus, please wake the fuck up, Sleeping Beauty.* "I'll call Jesse and see if he wants to come. Trey's too fucked up, so let's not even mention this shit to him right now." Turner dials and nibbles at one of his lip rings. "We could even invite Josh," he says, his grin getting a little more real, a little more Turner Motherfucking Campbell. "Oh, but that's right," he snaps his fingers, "he's not *of age* yet." Turner chuckles while he waits for Jesse to answer.

"If it's okay with you guys, I want to invite Kash and Wren to come out with us. They're not doing too well right now." Dax bends down and scrapes his smoke against the cement before dropping it back into a plastic baggy and tucking it into his back pocket. "While you guys have been chilling in your *mansion*," Dax bites the word off the tip of his tongue and rises to his feet, sharing a steely gray eyed glare with Turner, "we've been cooped up in a hotel, surrounded on all sides by fans, no *manager* to wipe our asses." The word *manager* slithers from his lips like a curse as he moves away and Sydney's eyes follow the movement.

"Shit," she whispers, and I don't disagree, watching Dax's back and wondering if I should extend my shepherding of wisdom outwards, into Amatory Riot. They might feel broken, but they're just getting started. All of this pain and angst and heartbreak, it'll only make the rock 'n' roll more real. If they can get through this, we'll have some serious competition on our hands.

I reach down and take Lola's fingers in mine, squeezing them and scooting close enough that the fine hairs on our upper arms brush. She shivers and my grip tightens.

"Thanks for this," she tells me, turning and pushing herself into me. My hands come around her waist, gentle at first, but pressing harder when her breasts squish into me. Our lips meet and I slide my tongue into her mouth, tasting her heat and smelling a sweet citrusy perfume on her clothes. The last couple of days, we've been sleeping in the same bed together, visiting Lydia, sitting by the pool, but we were both too busy trying to process everything that's happened. It didn't feel like we were really together. Right now, right here, in this moment it

DOLL FACE

does.

"No, thank *you* for putting up with all this shit, for visiting my daughter with me. To be honest with you, she scares me a little. If only because I don't know how to handle her. And every time we go over there, every time that she *doesn't* call me Dad, I feel like insides are going to spill out my belly button." Lola slides her hands up either side of my face as I stare into her shades and wish I could tear them away from her eyes and toss them into the street. Fucking sunglasses.

"Don't be scared of her, Ronnie. And don't thank me for being there. It's the least I could do. When *you're* ready, when you've embraced the idea of being a father, body and soul, and you've forgiven yourself for all the things you've done, that's when she'll call you by name. Until then, just be patient." Lola kisses me and my heart soars. Well, okay, that's not the only part of me flying a flag if you catch my drift. Lola slides her hands down my cheeks, over the tattoos on my throat, my arms, and then cups my junk, right there in front of Sydney and Turner who both wrinkle their noses in disgust. "And keep hold of this. You're gonna need it later. If I don't get laid sometime soon, my fucking head's going to explode." She leans up on her toes and kisses my cheek. "Better yours does first, if ya catch my drift."

We manage to convince Dax to come with us back to the mansion with promises from Wren and Kash to get a ride from their security detail over here. Seems like as good a meeting place as any, and we've got a few hours before the club opens. Fine by me. Lola and I have other ways of entertaining ourselves until it's time to head out. Or at least, we did until I walked in here and found Paulette Washington sitting in my living room with Milo Terrabotti.

I pause in the doorway and clear my throat, drawing his attention up and over to me. Milo hurriedly sets down his tea or coffee or whatever the fuck it is before coming over to me, dressed in his best suit and tie, hair perfect, the black bags under his eyes covered up with makeup.

"Mr. McGuire," he says with a smile as he takes my arm and guides me into the living room, towards the sofa where Miss Washington sits. She doesn't bother to stand up, lifting up a hand for me to shake. I do – briefly – and drop it like it's poisonous. When I glance over my shoulder, I see that I'm the only one in here. Lola told me

DOLL FACE

she was going to go *tart herself up* which I guess means she's going to dress for the occasion. The phrase puts a smile on my face that Paulette mistakes for something else when I turn back to her, beaming up at me like I've already said *yes* to whatever crazy idea it is that she's come up with.

"I'm guessing you dragged me in here because you know I'm not so high on smack anymore that I can't make my own decisions. I've now become the 'difficult' one." I make quotes with my fingers and feel bad when Milo cringes like a kicked dog. The poor guy's been through enough; I need to cut the bastard some slack. "Sorry. Long day." I almost mention the swab that got shoved up my piss hole but decide that's a topic better left for later, in case Paulette really pisses me off. I can whip that out and see if her skin crawls when I mention it. "What I mean to say is *no reality show.*" Paulette opens her mouth, but I'm not done. "When I say *no reality show,* I really mean *no fucking reality show.* Not now, not next month, never. It's too much."

"Mr. McGuire," Paulette says when I give her the chance, folding my arms over my chest and refusing to take the seat Milo offers me. When my manager realizes that I'm not going to sit, he sighs and makes himself comfortable on his feet behind me. "I can understand why you'd say that, given the recent *slew*," Paulette practically growls the word out, "of terrible reality television. Programs that are so far removed from reality that you'd be more likely to find truth in sitcom. Listen, Ronnie – can I call you Ronnie? – you're a smart man and obviously a very strong person to survive drug addiction. Many people – my own sister included – never make it out alive." She leans forward, folding her perfect hands on her black slacks. *Jesus, she reminds me of America.* I tilt my head to the side and study her face, her perfect nose, her perfect cheeks, her perfect chin. She's like a little brunette Barbie doll, all Beverly Hills plastic surgery and cosmetic decadence. Hmm. America, at least, was real – physically speaking. Still, the resemblance is enough to convince me that I don't trust this bitch as far as I can throw her. No way, no how. "But you should at least hear me out. The idea I pitched to the studio has got a lot of people talking. This is the next best thing in entertainment. Live, twenty-four hour feeds of the house via planted cameras. No camera crew, no interference, no cut away interviews. Just you and your families living here and interacting. When you leave the house, nobody will follow you. You'll still have your privacy."

"Yeah, just not at home, not in the one place in the

DOLL FACE

world that's *supposed* to be sacred. Sorry, lady, but I smell your shit from over here. You want us to sign away our lives, let you market our pain, our love, our sex, our friendship, whatever. My music, I can sell because I know it's going to fucking touch people *here*." I thump a fist against my chest. "But I won't sell my soul. That shit's just for rent, just up for a glimpse while we're onstage. Anything else would be a travesty."

"Mr. McGuire," Milo begins from behind me, but I wave him off. I don't need to consult with the boys about this, talk to my parents, discuss the pros and cons with Lola. I already have my answer and it's resounding in my skull like a lonely echo in the Grand Canyon. *No. No. No.*

"My daughters will be moving in here soon. The last thing they need is for their childhoods to be filmed, for their father's fuckups to be immortalized every second of every day. The answer is no."

"This could be the thing that separates you from today's news to tomorrow's Gods. The world won't be *allowed* to forget about Indecency. We'll have a website with live feeds, twenty-four hours a day, and pages filled with fact – straight from the horse's mouth. Your hopes, your dreams. You'll each have a blog to post every thought that flickers through your head to the world." I feel my lip wrinkle and have to really wonder if this woman is mentally challenged. How is she not getting this?

"I don't *want* my every whim broadcast to the world. And holy fucking fuck, the website thing? Is that meant to entice me? That's even *worse*. So not only are the cameras catching my every waking moment, but they're also playing them all. No cuts? No way to hide anything that happens here? You can *really* forget that shit."

Paulette seems unfazed. She's still smiling at me.

"We could negotiate a little. Say, no cameras in the bathrooms or bedrooms?" Paulette lets her lips curl at the corners. Her version of a smile is fucking terrifying. She sweeps brunette hair over her shoulder and flutters her lashes at me, not in any coquettish sort of way, but more like she's hinting at something unspoken, something I'm not getting. Awesome. More shit to slog through. I pinch my mouth tight and turn away, refusing to participate in this discussion any further. If the words *fuck no* don't mean anything to this woman, I have nothing else to say.

Milo calls after me, but I'm officially done here, starting up the stairs and heading for my bedroom. Paulette might stay and try to convince my manager, my

DOLL FACE

bandmates, whatever. They will *never* convince me, so fuck 'em. If I stay firm and say no, my friends will stand by my side. That's just the way we are; we work as a unit. Always have, maybe always will.

I open the door to my room and find Lola in a bright pink bra and panties, standing in front of a full length mirror, dancing to "Sex Metal Barbie" by *In This Moment*. The song gives me chills, especially when I see Lola's red lips mouthing the words, her fingers crawling down her side, teasing the waistband of her panties with her fingertips. *Holy shit.*

I step inside and shut the door behind me, flipping the lock before Paulette Washington decides to come looking for me. Lola doesn't notice me, running her fingers through her hair and moving with the music. Her bandages are gone, and I watch as she teases the wounds, tracing them and cringing a bit when she gets too close. As the song winds towards its end, the lyrics repeat the word *sex* over and over again, turning my rigid cock into steel. I could probably hold up a skyscraper with this baby. Jesus. Blue balls? I'm way beyond that. This is fucking *steel cock* and it's ten times as deadly.

"Hey," I say as the song finally fades away and Lola jumps in surprise, spinning and flinging one tattooed arm over her breasts, slapping her other hand over her pantie covered crotch. When she sees me standing there, she sighs and drops her guard, breathing out a sigh of relief.

"Holy-dooly," Lola breathes as I close the distance between us and pause, the toes of my boots less than an inch from her bare feet. "You scared the fucking shit out of me."

"Sorry, babe," I say, reaching down and placing my hands on her hips, feeling the warmth of her skin assaulting my senses and drawing even more blood into my painfully stiff cock. Lola looks down and then back up at me, a grin building on those red lips. Her eyes look even bigger, ringed in liner and shadowed with a shimmering gold color that emphasizes the brilliant blue of her irises. I keep trying to come up with something to accurately describe them, but nothing seems to fit. Cerulean simplicity. No, not quite right. A bite of brilliant sapphire, speckled with stars, ringed in Caribbean Sea.

Asuka pops into my mind, suddenly and without warning, but I don't flinch. I'm used to it.

Ronnie, when we're old and gray, will you still look at me like that, like I'm the most beautiful women that ever walked the face of the earth?

I swallow hard and watch as Lola catches on my pain,

DOLL FACE

mirrors it back in her own eyes.

I pull her against me, oh so gently. My body's aching with need, but my heart is pouring blood, and I just need a second. We both do.

"I need to call my dad," she mumbles, her lips moving against my T-shirt, her breath penetrating the cotton, warming my skin. I sigh and cup the back of her head with one hand, planting a kiss on her scalp before I pull away. Lola's staring at the rose on my T-shirt instead of my face, sliding her fingers down my bare arms and then adjusting her gaze with a raised eyebrow. "But maybe I should take care of that first?" she asks, flicking her eyes up to mine for a moment before reaching for my jeans. I smile softly and take her wrists in my hands, but I don't stop her. I just rub my thumbs in circles over her beating pulse as she unbuttons and then unzips my pants, the pain receding from her face like the tide, like I'm the Goddamn moon. The fact that I actually have the power to influence her mood doesn't escape me. *This could work, I think.* I mean, I know we're still missing those day to day interactions with one another, but I figure since we survived all the rough stuff, that shit should be easy.

Besides, I've fallen in love before. I know what it feels like when the trap door of your life opens underneath you and drops you, lets you tumble endlessly through the everyday and right out the other side to the bottom of the world. Welcome to fucking Wonderland, Alice. Just don't expect that you'll ever be able to leave. That whole *better to have loved than lost* bullshit? It's true. But once I felt that sting, it was like the worst kind of drug, one that you can't live without. I need another hit and Lola's gotta be it.

"Stop ruminating and let me touch your dick," she says, flicking me in the chest and giving me that stubborn, pouty expression that I like so much. I feel my mouth pull back into a grin and raise my hands in surrender, groaning as she finally frees my cock from the confines of my jeans. I don't know how Turner does it to be honest with you; my new pants aren't even close to as tight as his and I feel like my fucking balls are suffocating. Lola shoves my boxers down my hips and takes me in her hand a split second before the guilt kicks in and I find my body freezing up, my fingers curling into fists. "No," she says, wrapping her fingers around my shaft hard enough that she makes me grunt.

Our eyes meet and I feel a whisper of a smile cross my lips.

"Don't do that. Listen, buddy, I've let you play nursemaid for a whole week. It was great while it lasted,

… but I'm healed up enough that I can say this with complete and utter confidence: if you don't fuck the shit out of me, right here, right now, I will kick you right in the nuts and I won't apologize for it. What good does it do me to date a fertile rock God if he won't rock with his cock out every once in a while?"

"Hey, I'm not arguing," I whisper as she slides her hand down my shaft, gripping so tight that I have a hard time forcing the words out. "Especially if that's how you really see me. I was thinking *deadbeat dad* was a more accurate term for my iniquities." Lola scoffs and tightens her grip enough that I drop my hand to her forearms and grunt, the breath suctioned from my lungs with a single touch. Holy crap. Not only do I think Lola is the most rockin' chick I've ever met, but the lack of sex has left my skin hypersensitive. Her touch feels like molten fire as she works my body like we've known each other for ever, like she knows exactly where to touch. Either that or she's just that good.

"Shut the fuck up, Ronnie," Lola tells me, leaning forward and raising herself up to her toes, touching her lips to mine. That molten fire travels up my spine and into my limbs, into my mouth. I find the fingers of one hand curling in Lola's hair, the other sliding around her back and pulling her closer to me. Our tongues tangle together and I feel a frenzy wash over me, a desperate need to pick Lola up and slam her back into the wall of the sitting area, fuck her bareback and dirty, feel her wetness sliding over me. I moan and she growls back, pumping me harder, faster.

My left hand squeezes her ass, the supple flesh bulging between my fingers as I tighten my grip enough that she whimpers into my mouth. But she doesn't stop fucking my cock with her hand, doesn't stop kissing me with enough force to bruise. Unconsciously, I scoot us forward, pull her back with my hand on her hair and her ass. When Lola's back hits the wall and she grunts, I snap back into my senses a little. Condom.

"One sec, babe, one sec." Lola growls at me as I pull back and refuses to let go of my cock, keeping me hostage with her breasts heaving and a bead of sweat trailing between them, soaking into the bright pink fabric of her lacy bra. *Fuck me with a fat dildo.* How the hell am I supposed to say no to that? "I have to get a condom," I whisper as she drops to her knees, one hand still wrapped around my dick. My throat gets dry and I have a really hard time wetting my lips enough to speak. "One sec," I repeat, but Lola holds me tight, pumps me hard and draws pre-ejac from the tip of my cock.

"No. I'm tired of your whore jobs. Only prostitutes

DOLL FACE

put condoms on to blow dick, Ronnie."

"I'm just trying to protect you," I whisper back, wondering if there's anything in this world that's less sexy than freaking diseases. *Shit.* If I've stayed true to Asuka all these years, I'd have been ready for Lola, ready to start a life that didn't include tests and baggage and baby mamas and kids. But this is the hand I dealt myself, so I'm going to roll with it and play my best cards.

Lola ignores me, tracing the shape of her lips with the head of my cock. Pre-cum shimmers on her mouth and breaks down my pattern of logical thought. *Goddamn it.* I let my head fall back and rest my hands on her scalp, curling my fingers in that dark, dark hair of hers. It's perfectly straight, soft, teasing the whorls of my fingertips as I increase the strength of my grip in conjunction with the pressure of her mouth against my dick. Lola pauses to press a series of wet kisses down my shaft, squeezing my balls with her left hand before finally taking me into her mouth. She grips the base as she envelops my cock into the ardent blaze of her mouth.

Son of a bitch.

I feel my eyelids droop as my body sags with the pleasure, forcing me to move one hand from Lola's hair to the wall. This is the first time I've had the privilege of feeling her bare against my dick and it's fucking intoxicating. How am I supposed to make good decisions when my brain feels like it's been scraped out and fried up, shoved back and scrambled? Motherfucker.

Lola hums as she swirls her tongue around the head of my cock, paying special attention to the sensitive underside. With my thoughts virtually obliterated, the only image that runs through my addled brain is of throwing Lola over the bed and fucking her from behind, no condom, just my dick in her tight pussy. I mean, if her mouth feels this good …

Lola keeps a tight grip on the base of my shaft, slamming her mouth against her fist and deep throating my cock. My fate is fucking sealed and I groan, leaning over, putting my weight against my outstretched arm and using the wall for support as I come hard and fast, shooting a load deep into Lola's throat. My muscles tighten and then release, leaving me a melted frigging mess as she pulls away and visibly swallows. My eyes get caught on her throat, working to swallow my seed. I swear, I'm hard again by the time she gets to her feet.

"Not so bad, was it, mate?"

"Yeah, yeah, yeah," I whisper, wrapping my arms around her waist and shoving her into the wall. When we

DOLL FACE

kiss, I taste the saltiness of my body on her lips and feel a possessive growl rip through my throat. It feels wrong that I've been with other women without a condom when Lola and I are stuck here in this limbo, waiting for stupid frigging test results. Lydia should be *her* daughter; Phoebe should be. For the first time in forever, I imagine what it'd be like to get Lola pregnant, to actually stick around and see what the whole process is like, to hold my kid as soon as they take their first breath in this weird, twisted ass world. "Not so bad at all. I think I could handle that on a daily basis. Or hell, even two, three times a day if that's what it takes to make you happy."

I move my mouth to Lola's jaw, her ear, breathing against her hair as I work my kisses down her throat, across her collarbone. I bite at her taut nipples through the pink fabric, grazing my teeth against the tender flesh as she groans and wraps her arms around my neck.

"Depends on if you're a good boy or not," she whispers, and I smile, reaching back to unhook her bra. "As in, you better not be. I don't like good boys, Ronnie. I want you to be naughty." Lola shoves me back and wraps her arms over her chest to keep her suddenly loose bra in place. "Play a set for me," she whispers and I raise an eyebrow, glancing over at the kit in the corner of the room. Even when shit gets bad, even when the world's in a drooping funk around me, I miss the music if we're separated for more than a few days. When our shit got delivered the night before last, I dragged my kit up here and sat down to play, only nothing would come out. It was a miserable feeling, like I was too bogged down in details to just let go and listen to the beat.

"Right now?" I ask and she nods, leaning back against the wall and sliding her fingers down her belly, next to her gunshot wound, and into her panties. When Lola finds what she's looking for, her eyes get hooded and her breath softens.

"Play for me, baby. I want to hear your beat."

I smile and start towards the kit, pausing to fix my pants.

"If you're gonna do that, take your fucking shirt off. You already threatened to do it once today. Might as well go through with it." I grin and rip the fabric over my head, tossing it onto the ugly cream colored sofa that came with the house. Can't wait to replace that ugly ass shit.

I sit down at my throne and lick my lips, holding my sticks in tight fingers and closing my eyes. I can still taste Lola's mouth on mine, still feel her lips sliding down my shaft. I open my eyes back up and watch her

DOLL FACE

touching herself, staring back at me, waiting for me to make something out of nothing, to spin notes into feeling, to turn boring black and white marks on a page to reality. I bite my lower lip and tap my foot on the wood floor beneath my feet, getting a feel for the song I want to play. I run through an Indecency set list and decide on a pre-Asuka, pre-Travis tune, something that connects my soul to theirs.

I spin my sticks in my fingers and start to play.

At first the beat sounds a little lonely, like my drums are crying out for guitar, bass, for a voice to soothe their dark souls. But then I catch Lola's hooded gaze, watch those blue eyes spin with storms as she bites her lower lip and pleasures herself to the sound of my aching heart. Because that's what my music is to me, a reflection of the noise inside my soul, the frantic hammering of my heart against my ribcage. My anxiety. My hope. My fear. My dreams. I spin my sticks again and close my eyes. Don't need to see to play. Never have. Not even for this song, which is in 7/8 time signature.

Basically, the number and length of beats in each measure. If that doesn't make any sense, don't let it get to you. Who the fuck cares, right? The only thing that matters in music to me is how it makes me feel, how the pulse of the song matches the blood thrumming in my veins. And if I sound hippy-dippy to you, don't think it's because I wasn't taught right. My parents made sure I was brought up on the piano and then when I made the decision to switch to drums, they found me a teacher for that, too. I wonder if they ever look back on that decision and consider it a mistake? They shouldn't though, not really. If anything, it's the music that's kept me alive all these years.

I take a gasping breath and feel my arm muscles protesting, threatening mutiny for taking those two weeks off. It was the single largest break I've ever taken – barring Asuka's and Travis' deaths. I find myself getting lost in memories, seeing faces long gone and broken, so I force my eyes open, make myself count quarter notes to pull it all together.

One, two, three, four, five, six, sev.

There's no change in playing the hi-hat – that pair of cymbals off to the left, run by the foot pedal – but you can feel the difference on the bass drum and the snare. I keep counting, letting my lips move but refusing to speak a single word. Don't need to; my drums have voices. Each part of my kit is like a different entity, speaking to me in words and phrases, twisting its needs with my own, so we come out howling like a single demon instead of the chorus that we are.

DOLL FACE

Ghost notes on my snare drum give way to rim shots and then back again as the instrument responds to my emotions, as it feels my pain for the past and my hope for the future. Back and forth, I let it sing because there's nobody else around to do it.

Lola's hand moves quicker and she bites her lower lip so hard, I'm afraid she's going to make herself bleed. But I don't stop playing. I won't. Not until she wants me to.

I finish up my song, kiss the tip of my sticks, and start in on another. I have no idea what time we're supposed to go clubbing, but I don't give a fuck. If the others have to wait, so be it. When the devil calls, I come running, letting his demons prick me with their horns until I'm pouring sweat, tasting it on my lips, feeling it slick up my fingers. Doesn't stop me. I keep playing, hitting my kit hard, hoping the sticks turn to splinters in my hands, shards that can cut at the same time they can sing. I *want* that.

I use a heel-toe technique on my kick drum, a rocking movement that produces a double stroke. It's supposedly hard to do, but not for me. I'm not trying to brag, not trying to toot my own horn; this is just the way things are. If there's one place in my life that I've never struggled, that I've never screwed up, it's this.

Lola's voice rises in time with my playing, until she's shouting and sliding to the floor, a quivering pile of flesh and shuddering muscles, a pulsing heartbeat and sweat sprinkled skin that draws me like a moth to flame. I want to let myself fucking *burn*. I screw the rest of the song out, gritting my teeth and clenching so hard that one of my sticks really does *break*.

I stand up suddenly and chuck it against the wall, shoving my kit unceremoniously out of the way as I stomp across the carpet in my boots and slide my arms under Lola, fingers tight against her skin but gentle.

"Like I said," she whispers as I carry her to our ugly gold bedspread and lay her out on the king sized bed I never thought I'd have, that I'd end up sharing with another *drummer*. "Bloody brilliant." I lean down, nibble her earlobe and breathe a sigh of contentment against her throat. Sweat drips from my body onto hers as I slide my stick up her thigh and find her heat, pushing it inside as Lola gasps and arches her back.

"Now I'm going to play you like I play my drums," I growl out, letting that feral urge break over me. I mean *fuck it*. Why fight? I keep trying to hold myself in check, keep preparing for the worst, but isn't it already over? Yeah, sure I have some gumshoeing to do, some answers to discover, some bullshit to shovel, but I can relax for

DOLL FACE

this one, single, little moment, can't I? "Next time, it'll be your turn to play *me* something."

Lola starts to speak, but I cover her mouth with mine, fucking her with the slick piece of wood, the one that just made my kit sing, but is much, much happier here, drawing sounds from Lola's throat.

"More," she whispers, reaching down to grab my wrist, to graze her teeth across my lower lip. "I need more. Get that skinny stick out of the way and fuck me with your cock. Now." I raise an eyebrow and sit back, sliding the stick from her pussy and raising it to my mouth. Lola's eyes shimmer like sapphires and she raises an eyebrow. "You wouldn't dare." I slide the stick between my lips, tasting her heat, the sweetness of her body. Can't help myself. This is all her fault. *She's* the one that asked me to play. The music always wakes up all sorts of weird shit inside of me. Normally, I dull it back down with drugs. Today, I don't have that luxury. So if I'm thinking all kinds of weird shit – like how I'm going to marry this girl – you'll have to excuse me. I'm a drummer; it's what we do. And, like I said before, I had a chance with a soul mate and I lost it. Not many people get a second one. I refuse to waste it.

So I lick the stick and then fling it away, against the glass doors that lead out to the balcony.

"You're a nasty fuck, aren't you, Ronnie?" she asks me, sliding her hands up my sweat soaked abs, digging her fingernails into the grooves of my muscles. I smile down at her, tracing the leopard tattoo on her shoulder, the drum kit on her belly. Lucky for her, the bullet managed to avoid fucking up her ink. That'd have been a damn shame. I scoot back and lean over, running my tongue across the words *Sugar Baby* that are tattooed under her belly button. "Bloody fucking pervert."

"Only if that's what you want me to be," I whisper, looking up from under a fall of dark hair. I sweep it away and sit up again, unbuttoning my jeans. I pause at the zipper and scoot off the bed, retreating into the bathroom to dump out my duffel bag. Underneath all the drug paraphernalia are a handful of condoms, all with the Indecency logo of course. I'm definitely going to need some more, and very, very soon. Or at least until my test results come back. Then maybe Lola can get on the pill or whatever. Or shit, maybe I should get a vasectomy? As much as I'd love to see Lola pregnant with my baby, I already have four fucking kids. All under the age of seven. Ugh.

I cut those thoughts off at the source and jog back into the room to find Lola bent over, ass up in the air, stretching like a kitty cat. *Fuck.* Her panties are gone,

DOLL FACE

pussy swollen and ready for me, and my fingers itch to take hold of her hips and pound her like a snare drum.

"Hurry up, babe. Let's do it. This time, when I start screaming, there won't be any fucking cops to break down the door." She glances over her shoulder at me, brunette hair sliding across her back as she turns. I don't waste any time following her instructions, unzipping my jeans and sliding the condom down my cock which is already moist, drenched in sweat, saliva, pre-cum.

I climb up on the bed behind Lola, give her bullet wound a passing glance and push it from my mind. If something hurts, she'll tell me.

I put the head of my cock against her heat and she thrusts backward, impaling herself on my shaft as we both groan and collapse together, my balls slapping against her ass as I fuck the shit out of her. I don't hold back. Couldn't even if I wanted to.

"I want you to be mine, Lola," I tell her, voice quiet but intense. I can taste the desperation in my own words as our bodies slide together and her muscles clamp down tight, trying to make up for the bit of latex that's separating me from her wetness. I want to feel Lola all the fuck over me.

"I want to be," she whispers, digging her nails into the

bedspread, lifting her ass up for a better angle. I pound faster, fuck harder, thrust deeper. "Mark me, baby," she growls, rocking against me, matching my beat, grinding against me while her pussy clenches in a pulsing rhythm that feels like the world's best song sounds. I drop my head back with a groan, using my hands on Lola's hips to keep myself steady. And hey, if nothing else, this wild little fuck of ours is helping me to appreciate this expensive ass bed that we probably spent way too much on. *Fuck you, Paulette Washington, you and your cameras will never see a single second of this.* "Slap my ass," Lola commands in a screechy whisper, one that promises I'll get one of her epic little screams very soon.

"As you wish," I growl, raising my head back up and appreciating the view before I crack my palm against her cheek and her pussy flexes in response, milking the shit out of my dick. I slap her again, same response. Again, again, again. Until her ass is red and she's whimpering for more, telling me to pull her hair. I wrap my fingers in it and yank back, hard but not hard enough. *Shit, I can't wait until she's all healed up. God help her when she is. We'll be fucking like rabbits then. Each and every room of this house is gonna get some.*

"Don't stop, Ronnie," Lola snarls, slamming herself into me as I slap her ass again and enjoy the way it jiggles. *Fuck yes.* And then the screaming starts, and she's getting so tight I can hardly move inside of her. One of her tattooed arms slides underneath her body and goes for her clit, working it like a machine while I pump inside of her, praying and dreaming about the day I get to shoot my load into her fucking womb. "Ah, FUCK A NUN'S DRY CUNT, that's good," she moans and then screams, and then moans again.

When Lola comes, she washes my balls and thighs with her hot juices, drenching me as I keep thrusting, slamming her body into the bed while she whimpers and convulses beneath me, muscles tightening and drawing my own orgasm just a moment later.

I explode inside the condom, fill that baby up, and break it.

CHAPTER 11
LOLA SAINTS

"You're supposed to leave room in the tip," I tell Ronnie, flicking him in the junk and smoking my ciggy with post coital satisfaction curling in my belly. *Oh yeah, that was nice.* Shit, after so long, a boring little missionary screw in the dark would've felt like heaven. But that was so much better. There's nothing I love more than watching Ronnie fuck his drums before he fucks me. A good rut is like gold to me, baby.

"I *did* leave room in the tip," he says, still sounding a little freaked out. Looks it, too, with his eyes gettin' all buggy. The thick slashes of eyeliner don't help, making his brown eyes look almost as big as mine. "I don't know what happened."

"You came like a cow and blew a rubber? What the fuck, Ronnie?" Turner says, appearing out of nowhere and pausing next to us with his hands on his hips. At night, the entire property here glows with well-placed lights, strung through the trees and wrapped around the bases of imported palms. It's almost too perfect. I get the chills and have to pinch my own arm to remind my addled brain that I actually live here.

"Shut up, Turner," he growls, looking fierce for a minute there, getting my poor pussy all wet again. Good thing I wore the soft black panties, one of the few pairs of mine that managed to make it to the mansion. These babies will catch all the happy juices and keep things clean downstairs. I finish my cigarette and drop it on the ground, using my new fuzzy pink heels to crush it out. *Maybe* I shouldn't be tottering around like a stork in these four inch tall little lovelies, but I can't help it. Lola Rubi Saints is not a wearer of flats, sneakers, sandals, or anything in between. I get that heels are kind of sexist, a little ridiculous, totally impractical. Fuck it.

I paired the shoes with black skinny jeans and an Amatory Riot T-shirt in pale blue. Tore off the shoulders and cut the holes in my pants myself – it can be done, kids. Ronnie said I looked *motherfucking fly,* so I guess I did good. I even let him clean and patch my wounds up, loaded myself on painkillers, and stuck my very last plastic bottle of vodka in my pocket. I figure it's okay to drink, provided I'm doing it to have a good time and not just drown my worries. Bottoms up, bitches.

"This is serious shit right here," he snaps at his friend, but Turner looks unfazed. He's smiling at his friend, at me, at the van pulling up the driveway, presumably with Kash and Wren inside of it. "I really wanted to get those test results back first," Ronnie adds in a hushed whisper. I put a hand out and squeeze his arm while Turner rolls his eyes and runs his tongue over his silver lip piercings.

"Oh my God, dude, chill the fuck out. Your usual late night groupie consisted of virgins and squeaky clean coeds. I don't know how you did it, but you always picked the clean ones out. If anybody has room to worry, it's Jesse. I mean, fucking Rook Geary? That's frigging sick."

"You are such an asshole, man," Jesse says, appearing in a black tank and jeans, boots and a similar style of makeup to Ronnie and Turner. It's like the whole band has a *look* that they're going for. "You don't think I bagged it when I fucked Rook?"

"You mean when he fucked you, right?" Turner snorts

DOLL FACE

as he gets out a cigarette and lights it before reaching a hand into his tight girly pants and adjusting his junk. "Sorry, Lola," he says, wrinkling his nose up like he finds it amusing and not like he's actually sorry at all, "but sometimes when you tuck, shit gets stale up in there."

"Christ," Ronnie snorts, blowing smoke in his friend's face while Jesse shakes his head and scowls, running his hand through his short hair. Trey appears a moment later, following Sydney and Dax in his wheelchair and pausing at the top of the steps. He doesn't look particularly thrilled about our plans for a night out.

"Hope you guys enjoy yourselves while I rot away in here," he calls out. Turner pulls his hand from his pants and flips his friend the bird before straightening his bright blue tee that says *Untouchable* on it. Fits the situation somehow.

"Go jack yourself off to the Tattoo Terror website your sister's supposed to star on again. You don't want to blow too fast when you actually find a girlfriend. Get that practice in there." Jesse chuckles, but Trey just picks up a decorative vase near the front door and chucks it down the driveway at Turner. The white pieces scatter like seashells across the bricks while Turner laughs and slides nimbly out of the way. "That probably cost like five hundred bucks or some shit." He points at his friend with a hand covered in paw prints and bats, spider webs. "It's coming out of your share of the royalties." I glance back and catch Trey rolling his eyes before he wheels himself back inside and slams the door. Poor bloke. I know if I was stuck here in bed or in a chair, I'd be having some tantrums of my own.

"You're in a good mood," Ronnie comments as he looks first at Turner and then over at me, letting his eyes slide to mine again. I know he wants to keep obsessing about the wild sperm that managed to break down our defenses, but I'm okay. Granted, I find out he gave me a disease and I'll kill 'im. For now, everything's going to be alright. I'll get some morning after pills tomorrow and we're golden.

"Yeah, well, I got a call from the hospital and they've agreed to have Naomi moved to the mansion." Turner grins big as he says this, squinching his eyes up like a kid at Christmas.

"That's beaut, mate," I say and Turner lifts up his hand for a high five. I slap him one and he does this stupid little jig in a circle, flinging his cigarette up in the air in celebration. "When they bringin' her over here?"

"Day after tomorrow. Provided, of course, that I can get a full-time nurse to look after her. Shouldn't be a

DOLL FACE

problem though. I mean, who *doesn't* want to work for us, right?" I turn and glance at Sydney over my shoulder, watching as she approaches the van in her tight purple dress and black heels. Her blonde hair hangs over her shoulders in soft waves, and her makeup glitters in the glow of the white lights. If Dax doesn't go for her now, he's a fucking idiot. What's he got to lose? I keep watching as she smiles, reaching out a hand and letting somebody pull her inside ahead of Dax before poking her head back out and shouting at Turner.

"Campbell, we're following you guys, so don't get us lost, okay?"

"Got it, bitch," he says, turning towards the already open door of our van with a smirk. Leather seats, champagne, security guards that have already promised to wait outside the club for us. Has to be a good night, right? I look at the dude nearest us. These guys are all money and professionalism, not like Brayden's people who'd flat out refuse to get the fuck out of wherever it was that you asked them to leave. Not a moment's peace with those people and what do we have to show for it? A dead sister. Friends in comas. A gunshot wound that still hurts when I twist the wrong way. Assholes.

I start towards the van, but Ronnie reaches out a hand and grabs me. When I look at him, he has that gravely serious expression on his face. Before he can say anything and ruin the moment, I spin in his grip and raise myself up on my toes for a kiss. Lightning crackles between us, electrocuting me from my head down to my toes. Hope my hair's not sticking up every which way as I pull back and smile.

"Don't mention it again. Condoms break. Shit happens. Relax. Let's just enjoy ourselves tonight, okay?" Ronnie looks at me for a long, long moment before nodding and climbing in the van behind me.

XXX

Slick's looks like your usual dump of a bar from the outside, unremarkable inside. It's only after we abandon our security detail at the chain in the back, pass the first bodyguard and enter into a dark den of iniquities that I see anything special. *Holy fuck.* There's a long bar, entirely occupied by people in suits and long dresses, leather jackets and jeans, even surf shorts and tanks. Every type of person imaginable is in here, but they've all got one thing in common: they're engaged in some pretty

DOLL FACE

fucked up shit. People are snorting lines, slamming dope, even fucking in some of the high backed booths nearby.

Turner breezes right past of all of this and straight to the men's restroom, pausing to look over his shoulder at one of the booths. The skin around his mouth gets tight and his eyes flash with pain before he schools his expression and turns back, opening the bathroom door and ushering us all inside. It's a tight fit, but we manage, waiting patiently as he opens one of the stall doors. Somehow, I expected it'd be a hell of a lot more difficult to find this secret door but Turner makes it look like a piece of piss, grabbing a silver ring and pulling up a door to reveal a set of stairs.

"Well, fuck me runnin'," I say as Sydney cracks a tinnie she snatched off one of the tables on her way by. The people making out in the booth didn't even notice. She chugs the beer and then shakes her head, pointing at me.

"Took the words right out of my mouth. This is fucking weird, Turner."

"Are you sure this is legit?" the blonde guy from Amatory Riot asks. Kash, I think it is. He has his arm around this pretty little ranga, her bright crimson hair curled up on the top of her head in a knot. She snuggles into him with a sigh, and I can see that there's love between them. It burns like a fiery aura, like I can see colors swirling in the air around them. Or maybe that's just the sex talking. Having a naughty before I came out was a good move, put me in a chipper mood. I slip my little vodka bottle out and unscrew the top, offering it to Ronnie first before pouring the rest down my throat. I toss the plastic bottle in the rubbish bin as warmth explodes from my belly and climbs up my throat, setting my entire body on fire. *Ah, and now I remember exactly why this was my drug of choice.*

"Trust me," Turner growls, stepping back and gesturing with his hand, "this is fucking legit. Now get your asses down there and thank me later. Chop, chop, we ain't got all day." Jesse moves forward first, descending into the darkness a split second before Ronnie grabs my hand and pulls me along with him, down the steps and into a tunnel with white lights lining either side of the floor.

A giggle breaks from my throat, part nervousness, part vodka, part that bottle of champagne I downed on our way over here. Ronnie squeezes my fingers in his and pulls me close, around a corner and towards a pulsing blue glow and the strong, heavy beat of music. Some electronica crap is playing right now, but it doesn't really

DOLL FACE

matter. At this point, just the idea of a night out, a chance to taste reckless abandon and pretend that I'm *not* a murderer, that I didn't lose my sister in some crazy fucked up custody battle, sounds like heaven.

I close my eyes and listen to Ronnie's pulse, thrumming through his hand and into my body, up my arm and straight to my heart, like I've just slammed some pure, clean dope and it went straight to my chest. I suck in a deep breath, taste the distant hint of sweat and alcohol that lingers in the air.

"I'm sorry about the condom," Ronnie whispers, and I open my mouth to chastise him. He cuts me off with a growl. "Sorry that I didn't fuck you bareback when I had the chance." I shiver and lick my lips.

"Well, now that we're engaged and all, I suppose you'll be getting the chance to do that more and more often." Ronnie snorts as we come around another bend in the hallway and pause at a second set of stairs, this one leading into a massive warehouse, complete with pearlescent wallpaper and chandeliers, exposed ductwork and a throng of throbbing people.

"I'm sorry I said that." He pauses as we take our first step, right behind Jesse. The music swells and surges, like a tsunami, drowning me in the dying embers of the last song and filling my gently parted lips with the wicked fast beat of the next. "Well," he shouts, leaning close to my ear, helping me down the stairs in my heels, "not sorry that I suggested it, but sorry that it came out that way. You deserve better."

I don't say anything, just let my lips twitch in amusement as we pause near the bouncer and he studies us carefully, pausing on Ronnie like he's the straw that broke the camel's back, and pulling aside the chain to let us in. I glance over my shoulder and catch sight of Sydney and Dax. Amatory Riot's drummer doesn't look so good. He's got dark bags under his eyes, drooping lips, twitching fingers. I hope to hell Sydney really is interested in him as a man because he could sure use a woman in his life.

I turn back to the crowd and allow Ronnie to act as my shield, wrapping his arms over my shoulders, draping his big body across mine to keep gyrating hips and pointy elbows away from my injuries. It's kinda cute, ya know? Having him protect me like that. Last guy I was with was more inclined to actually *cause* serious injury rather than defend me from it. *Fuck you, Cohen. I hope you rot in hell, get resurrected, and have it happen all over again.*

"For the first time in my life, I'm not irritated that I'm so small or that the guys around me are so fucking big." I

DOLL FACE

lean my head back, letting Ronnie's chin scrape across my scalp. He leans into me as we work our way to the bar. "You are drinking with me tonight, right?" I ask as he helps me onto a stool and turns to glance over his shoulder. His muscles remain tense until he spots Turner, fighting towards us and slamming his side into the bar with a deep breath. It takes a second but once people start to realize who we are, the stares begin. Granted, nobody tries to molest us, and the stares are coming from famous faces, but still. Even here ...

"You hear that gnarly shit?" Turner asks, pointing up at the ceiling. I notice Ronnie visibly relaxes when his friend's in sight. "Not as good as our stuff, but still impressive." Turner spins and puts his back to the bar, facing out at the crowd. Most of the rubberneckers turn away, but I see a few girls biting their lips, exchanging glances, wondering if they can get the famous bad boy into bed. I wrap my fingers around Ronnie's bicep. He might not be the lead singer, but I know he's never had trouble filling his bed before. If I have to, I will piss all over him and mark my territory.

"Ronnie," I repeat and he turns to me, stepping closer, putting his hands possessively on my hips. "You are drinking with me, right?" His brown eyes find mine, searching them for a moment before he nods. I let a grin split my face and turn to the bartender. "Do you know what a Cherry Tootsie Pop is?" I ask and then decide to add, "and I ain't talkin' about the lollies." I've done my fair share of partying in the past, and I know how localized and scattered drink recipes can be. At this point in my life, I'm more than happy to grab the fucking bottles and mix it myself. The woman behind the bar leans in towards me, eyes sparkling. She's excited to see us here. That's good. Maybe we'll actually be able to get some good service tonight.

"I don't, but I can look it up," she shouts, tapping her pink nails on the countertop.

"Don't bother. It's all up here." I point at my head and then hold up a hand, lifting fingers as I name ingredients. "Chocolate vodka, Red Bull, grenadine. Give us a couple rounds to start, babe." I gesture absently at Ronnie and Turner and reach for my pocket, to grab the cash I stuffed there earlier. I might've gotten the pink slip from Ice and Glass, but I still made heaps of cash while I was at it. Ronnie grabs my wrist gently, drawing my fingers from my pocket and tossing some green on the counter next to me.

A moment later, he pulls me back, letting me turn in his arms until we're chest to chest.

DOLL FACE

The music switches to a jumpy pop song, from that blonde bitch, Cameron Koons.

Never bite the hand that feeds, baby. I got all you need to eat. I'm a glorious feast, so hop to this beat and BANG. BANG. BANG. With me. BANG, baby. BANG. BANG. BANG.

"I fucking hate her bloody songs, but they are catchy, yeah?" Ronnie chuckles and then pauses, looking at Turner over my shoulder. I pause and follow his line of sight, certain that he's never going to relax if he's this worried about his friend. *Oh. Holy shit.* Turner slams all three of the red shots lining the counter, faster than our poor bartender can make more. He coughs and leans over the bar, slumping onto my abandoned stool like the weight of his body's too much for him to hold up.

"You alright, bro?" Ronnie asks, but Turner just gives him this look of sheer misery. We scoot back a bit, trying to see if it's even possible to talk to one another with Cameron Koon's song pounding in our ears.

This is. Your time. To BANG. BANG. BANG. With me, baby.

Bass pulses through the concrete floor, shooting straight up my heels and making my entire body twitch as my muscles tighten and my spine twists, desperate to get moving. But poor Turner, poor fucking Turner.

"This is like déjà vu, bro. So bad. The song, the Red Bull, the club. I can't stop thinking of Naomi. Maybe it was a bad idea to come here?" Ronnie and I exchange a glance, and I step back, taking a spot on Turner's right while Ronnie heads up the left. I stand there and rub his back in circles while Ronnie tries to comfort him enough that we can be sure he won't run off and OD in the bathroom. Or grab one of the many eager faces around us for a quick little naughty. Not that I really think he'd do that, but sometimes people act weird when their life's in turmoil.

"She's going to make it, Turner. You gotta stay positive and fight through this. If the club's too much, we can have one of the vans take you back to the house." Turner shakes his head and snatches the next shot that our bartender places on the counter. He downs it as I reach for my own and follow suit. *Perfection.* Tastes like a chocolate covered cherry. Brilliant. Ronnie grabs his own shot and drinks, giving me a look over his friend's back.

"Nah, I'm cool." Turner reaches into his back pocket and comes up with a plastic bag filled with the powdery white perfection of blow. *Shit.* I force my gaze away, back towards the heaving crowd. It's almost as crazy in here as it is during one of our concerts. Almost. "I've got Snow White to keep me company." He tosses the bag on the counter and nobody blinks. Two seats down from me, there's a girl with a fucking needle in her arm. I guess the boys in blue overlook this club, probably with a lot of gentle, green persuasion. I wonder who owns the place?

"Turner, you're a big fucking boy, so I'm not going to try to tell you what to do, but," Ronnie puts his hand on the plastic bag, "if you're going to do this, do it, but please don't take it so far that I have to call an ambulance. Don't pull any Romeo and Juliet shit on me and pass out right when Naomi wakes the fuck up, you got it?" Turner rolls his eyes, but I can tell he's listening.

"Yeah. Whatever. Look, I had the best night of my life a few weeks ago, and it all started in this fucking club. Go play with Lola while you have the chance." Turner pauses, and I can tell he feels like the mood's getting too serious. "She'll probably be pregnant soon enough anyway, and you'll lose your chance." Ronnie smacks his friend in the back of the head and then steps away, holding out a hand for me.

"Sorry about that," he whispers into my ear, his lips moving against my skin, breath warm as it stirs my hair. "I've just never … seen him like this before. I don't want Turner to lose his happiness. I know how that feels."

Ronnie exhales deeply and then stands straight, sliding his hands down my side. His mouth twitches, and I can tell he wants to ask if I'm okay, but he bites back the question, listening to my body as I start to move against him, letting the beat work its way into my blood.

"No worries, Ronnie. You know I like the fuck out of your face," I say, poking him in the nose and then sliding an arm around his neck as our bodies start to sway with the wave of the crowd.

"I love the fuck out of yours," he tells me, and my body goes hot from head to toe. Our mouths connect, and I do my best to make him forget about the broken condom. I have a feeling that if he fixates on it, I won't get laid again for another two weeks. *Ugh*. These nice guys and all their silly morals and obligations.

I slide my tongue against his, tasting the sweetness of the shot, feeling the burn of alcohol in my limbs, swimming straight up to my brain. We kiss, even as the crowd begins to hop to another pop song. Our bodies move along with the mass of people until our mouths break apart with the motion and we dance with the group, letting the collective whole of the souls around us decide what movements we should make. As long as we're together, that's all that matters.

DOLL FACE

Out of the corner of my eye, I catch sight of Sydney and Dax. She's moving with the music, gyrating and spinning, blonde hair tinted blue from the flickering lights overhead. Dax moves with her, but I can tell he's off his guts, totally fried. Poor guy.

I turn my attention back to Ronnie, just enjoying his company, the touch of his hands on my hips, the sweat dripping down his forehead. We manage to make it through three songs before the bar calls and we end up on either side of Turner again, ordering another round of drinks – buttery nipples this time, baby. After we finish these, I get us all blow jobs and no, I don't mean the usual dick sucking kind. These little bites of perfection are made with Bailey's Irish Cream, Kahlúa, and a squirt of bright white whipped cream on the top.

"Doesn't taste half as good as you did this afternoon," I shout at Ronnie and laugh as Turner shakes his head in disgust and lays out two lines of coke, snorting them up in quick succession. He offers both Ronnie and me some, but we exchange a look and decide to pass. I know my limits. I can drink recreationally, sure, but if I start on the other stuff, I won't make it a week before I'm back in the bathroom with a little crystal to keep me company. "You want to dance with me?" I ask Turner, but he shakes his head, waving Ronnie and me off again.

We rejoin the crowd just in time to get a glimpse of a few figures moving across the stage that lines the entire back wall of the club. Just a few minutes ago, it was covered in people, dancing and making out and God only knows what else. Now it's empty but for a few folks in jeans, dragging equipment onstage like the best of roadies, hooking up speakers, setting a microphone center stage. Two guitars and a bass later, and there's a distinct buzz in the crowd, whispered voices and rumors coming faster than a teenage boy with a copy of his mum's *Victoria's Secret* catalogue.

Ronnie and I exchange a look a split second before a girl in a skintight aqua dress appears, the sparkles on her outfit gleaming like scales under the sudden spotlight that highlights her blonde form, turning her pale hair into a halo that's at complete odds with her wicked smile.

"Evening bitches," she says and then chuckles, tugging her dress down in the front with one hand and holding her mic with the other. The crowd murmurs appreciatively, like they're excited to see her but not particularly impressed. I guess that's what happens when you perform for celebrity royalty, eh? "My name is Cameron Koons and I'll be entertaining you all for a little while." Another laugh, one that's as fake as that smile. A band appears from offstage, moving like shadows behind

DOLL FACE

the leading lady. I feel a scowl twist my lips. They might as well be invisible. Nobody cares who they are or why the beat that Cameron's singing to is twisting their soul, shattering their faces, making them bounce and dance across the floor. *God, I hate soloists.* Music as a solo act? Hah.

I let my head fall back and stare at the exposed ductwork high, high above us.

Ronnie reaches down and squeezes my hand, bending down to whisper in my ear.

"Another drink?" he asks and I groan.

"Oh, hell yes. I don't know if I can continue to have a good time with that bitch onstage otherwise." I drop my chin back down and watch as a man joins Cameron, his shaved head gleaming in the lights, sunglasses on his face. When they start their first song off rapping together, I know I'm in trouble. Yuck. "Couple rounds of vodka shots never hurt anything, right?" I ask and Ronnie laughs.

I let him keep hold of my hand while we work our way back towards the bar. With Cameron onstage at the opposite end of the room, it doesn't take much effort to work our way back towards Turner who's scowling and shaking his head.

"I swear, I can't get away from this woman," he growls as Sydney and Dax appear to our left. Sydney helps Dax onto a stool and lets him slump to the counter, wiping a hand across her sweaty brow and pinching her lips with worry.

I got this booty, booty and I'm gonna shake it til you blow your goody goodies. Never drove so fast in the backseat of a car, never danced so hard to such a sick ass beat. I'm gonna move it til you recognize my skill, boy, and I'm gonna fake it til I make it, okay, 'kay?

"This has got to be the worst song I've *ever* heard," Sydney says, ordering up a round before I get the chance to. She tosses some cash on the counter and then runs both hands down her face. In the background, the rap finally dies away and the drums start up, shaking the walls and the floor, commanding how high the crowd jumps, how fast it pulses. Doesn't anybody realize here that Cameron Koons isn't making magic all on her own? I fucking hate pop stars.

"Bloody bush pig," I mumble under my breath, tipping back my shot. Cameron's voice rises to a crescendo just before she breaks off and the guitarist launches into a weak little solo that's actually enough to set the crowd off like a frog in a sock. Hmm. Oh well. Who am I to judge, right? I slam another shot back and

DOLL FACE

take a deep breath. The alcohol's just starting to get into the cracks of my brain, loosen up my muscles, push a slight smile onto my face.

"They're only excited to listen to this crap because they haven't heard a *real* musician perform live."

"Oh no," Ronnie says, reaching out and taking hold of his friend's upper arm. The two of them exchange a look. "Don't you dare do anything that *I'll* regret come morning. No fucking way. Without Naomi here, it's my job to keep you in line, Arkansas."

"Fuck off," Turner says, pushing back at Ronnie and rising to his feet. "I'm just going to pay a visit to the shitter, okay? No big deal." Ronnie releases Turner reluctantly but watches him carefully as he pushes his way through the crowd with the false bravado of a cocaine high. *Lucky bastard.* I reach out a hand for Ronnie's and take hold of his warm fingers, dragging him back into the crowd and letting him wrap his body around me. I'm at that tipping point between *drunk off my ass* and *still horribly alert.* I just gotta let the alcohol work its way through my blood, just like a good song, something that can be played over and over and over again.

I push my body into Ronnie's with force, find his

hands traveling over my ass, his forehead pressing against mine as we grind and sway with Cameron Koons and her puppet band. Ronnie's fingers slide along the waistband of my pants, warm my flesh with the slight brush of his, searing my skin as he teases me and smiles while he's doing it.

"You fucking asshole," I growl at him, leaning in close so I can put my lips against his ear. "If you're going to tease, you better damn well deliver. One more dry spell and you'll really get to see what my dad and sister used to call the *Crazy Banana Bender.*" I pause and suddenly the situation doesn't seem quite so funny. My body slows and the burning flames I felt for Ronnie sputter out in an instant. *Poppet*. My chest tightens and I have to swallow three times to get past a lump in my throat.

"Oh, doll face," Ronnie says, pulling me against him, sliding his hand over my hair and tucking me under his chin. "It'll be okay. We'll fight through this." I close my eyes and let the strong bass beat reverberate in my bones. That's the thing about grief, I guess. It comes and goes and no matter how hard you try to fight it, eventually it'll getcha. *Fuck.* I sniffle and pull back a bit, just enough that I run my arm across my eyes and shake my head.

"I feel like a fucking tool," I say, blinking suddenly

… and shaking my head. My booze-y brain swims as I sniffle again and glance back at the stage, watching Cameron as she basically fucks the stage, sliding across it in her ugly arse sparkly dress, licking her microphone like a shitty Turner Campbell wannabe. I switch my gaze back to Ronnie and close my eyes against a sudden surge of emotion when he cups my face in his hand. "I'm a coward, Ronnie. For days now, I've been avoiding calling my dad. I mean, I guess he probably already knows about Poppet, but *I* have to talk to him. Why am I here, drinking and dancing, when I should be doing that?"

"You can't punish yourself every second of everyday," Ronnie whispers, pressing his lips against my forehead, my cheek, my lips. "I've been watching you do it for weeks now, ever since Stephen showed up at the hospital that day. You *can* relax, Lola. It's *okay* to have a good time, even if you're grieving. The point of living through the tragedy is to actually *live*. You're a brave woman, even if you don't know that."

"Pig's arse!" I snort and Ronnie laughs, pulling me close, enveloping me in his arms and the warm, masculine scent of his body. He smells like lilies and soap, but I could just be imagining the first part, thinking of that tantalizing little tattoo under his shirt. I close my eyes for a second and let us loose ourselves in the middle of that massive crowd. I know, I know, a nightclub seems like a pretty fucked up place to have a moment like this, but that's life, babe. Uncontrollable, unpredictable, downright fucking bizarre. "I ... " I almost say the words *I love you,* but the song dies down and the crowd explodes with wild murmurs, drawing my attention up and over to the stage.

"Fuck." Ronnie's already looking that way, his mouth slightly parted, silver fillings glinting with the change in lighting overhead. The room darkens and a second spotlight appears on the stage. Only it's not the rapper dude in the sunglasses that's now up there with Cameron Koons, it's Turner Campbell. Well, fuck me runnin', that little asshole.

"Yo, yo, yo, Los Angeles," he slurs, slamming his boots across the stage and pausing not five feet from an absolutely thrilled Cameron. Her pink tinged lips curl into a grin and her eyes shimmer. Even from back here, I can tell she's ecstatic about the change in the program. Gazes flicker our way, and even in the throng of people, it's suddenly not so hard to spot Jesse, Sydney, Dax, Wren, Kash. Lovely. "I just want to give a shout-out to my fiancée." Ronnie groans here and shakes his head. "Naomi Knox," Turner raises his hand and the crowd

DOLL FACE

starts to titter, like a bunch of bloody birds in a tree, a flock that's just spotted a worm, "I love you, baby. I just want you to know that." Turner sniffles and looks over at Cameron.

"The lead singer of Indecency everyone." She holds her hand out to indicate Turner's scowling face and then looks over her shoulder at her band, nodding her chin like this is something she expected. Interesting. "As you well know, their song *One Woman* just surpassed my single *Belittle* on the Billboard charts, so congratulations are in order." She claps and the crowd follows suit, just as we hear the opening notes to said song.

Crap.

Only, this version of the song is like something you'd find in a cheap children's jewelry box. Open the top folks and listen to the cruddy little jingle within, stripped of soul and passion and heart. My teeth hurt as the guitarist's weak chords spring to life and Turner snarls into the microphone. All around us, California's elite start to exchange glances and the room goes still and silent for a split second, right before he says, "you want to see me fuck this stage up? So be it."

And then everything goes nuts around us.

People push towards the stage, shoving us forward,

encouraging us to join Turner as he lets loose with a massive scream, bending over at the waist and completely and utterly annihilating the sound of the instruments behind him. Whereas Trey or Naomi could compete with their guitars, where Ronnie could guide his friend's voice with a well-placed rim shot, these guys can barely keep up. I watch as Turner completely skips the intro to the song and goes straight for the meat of it.

"MYONEWOMAN! She's the ONLY one that understands. That fucking UNDERSTANDS."

Turner's powerful scream trails off into a gut wrenching sort of angry sob. Oh, and it's bloody beautiful. *Shit.*

"That mega fucking douche *bitch*," Ronnie snarls, pulling me against him and fighting the push and pull of the crowd, guiding us towards the edge of the room, hiding us in the shadows under the soffit near the restrooms. Even with the weakness of the music, Turner's voice carries the song and sends my heartbeat racing. The emotion in his words twists the song and flips it up to a whole new level. Oh how I'd like to see him sing like this *with* his actual band. What a fucking treat that would be.

Turner swings the mic around and spins, licking his

lips and crouching low at the front of the stage. His tight jeans stretch across his crotch as he spreads his knees wide and lets everyone take a look at what he's packing.

"She's the only one that breathes life into this *desolate*," he bites this word off, letting his eyes search the crowd's collective face, "hell hole. This desolate slice of *shit*. My one woman. My ONLY Goddamn motherfucking beautiful ugly bleeding bloody dark and BROKEN and whole and PERFECT FUCKING woman." Ronnie and I exchange a glance at the modified lyrics and watch as the polished gem of sin before us morphs into a growling beast, just as prone to being fucked by a good slice of rock 'n' roll as the rest of us. Celebrities? Eh. Heiresses? Screw 'em. Actors? Just people.

My pulse flutters as I watch the crowd eat Turner's voice up, taste his pain, flick their tongues out for just a sliver of that drama. Must be nice to have a life so perfect that you're willing to eat up the suffering of others just to feel human.

"Now what?" I ask Ronnie, glancing over at him. He's looking up at his friend, but there's nothing he can do at this point, not a Goddamn thing. "Another drink?"

"Yes," he murmurs, turning his brown eyes back to

mine, "yes, please."

CHAPTER 12
≈ Ronnie McGuire ≈

Turner won't get off the fucking stage, so I stop worrying about it by letting Lola order me another drink with a nasty sounding name. I feel totally off my game right now – it's been a long time since I was just *drunk*. It's a different feeling for sure. Better though, I think, less soul altering and more like I'm just physically fucked up.

I sway with the music, listening to my friend's voice rise and fall in steady rhythms around Lola and me, my hands on her hips, my cock rigid and unyielding between us. *That bastard.* I know what she wants as she slides her hands up my shirt and convinces me to keep the worries at bay for just another couple of moments. Weird how that works, right? One of us can be having a freak-out while the other stands by calmly and then bam, we're switching places. But that's a good thing, right? Like a fucking sign that this could really work between us.

"Take me in the bathroom and fuck me," Lola whispers as the crowd crashes the stage and we sit back here, bobbing in the smaller waves. I feel her mouth on my throat, her breath stirring my hair. *Fuck.* The whole broken condom thing is a fiasco I definitely don't want to repeat, especially not until after I get my test results back. And then we've got to deal with the whole birth control thing. Even though Turner was joking on his way over here, saying that Lola was probably already pregnant, he's got a point. Tomorrow morning, Lola and I will have another grown-up talk. Much as I fucking hate those. It almost feels like I've been avoiding them for so long that they're all catching up to me at once. Ugh. "Or better yet, slam me into the wall, right here. Do me bare and nasty, Ronnie." I bite my lip as Lola grabs at my waistband and tries to steer me in the direction she wants me to go.

It works.

Fuck, I mean, I'm weak and I'm a dude. Two things working against me. I couldn't stop right now, not even if I wanted to. The last little bit of me that wants to protest

DOLL FACE

is broken down by the booze and I find myself promising that tonight, it's okay. We can deal with all the rest of this shit tomorrow. Anyway, my dick doesn't really care about any of that, so he's happy with this plan. More than happy. *Thrilled.* Can't really blame him though. Who *wouldn't* want a woman that's willing to jump into a brand new relationship, take on a pair of kids from other women, sit with my tight-lipped parents in their suburban home without batting an eye? And I mean, I get that Lola was a part of Stephen's plan, but I don't blame her for it, not for any of it.

"Right here, Ronnie," she tells me, spinning us around so that her back's against the wall, her legs around me, her fingers threaded together behind my neck. I lean down to kiss her, starting slow, mimicking Turner as his rapidly slurring voice twists through the microphone. People in the crowd keep bringing him drinks and he keeps taking them. I should probably get over there and deal with it but for once, I just want to enjoy *my* moment, just be happy for *me*. I figure if I can hear him singing through the mic, he's not doing anything else that might get him into trouble. That'll have to be enough.

Ronnie McGuire is currently occupied.

I increase the intensity of my kiss, trying to take some pleasure in the raw, undisciplined beat of the drums from onstage. Our slick tongues slide together, teeth scraping against one another, fingers grasping. Mine knead Lola's flesh in a greedy grip, not oblivious to the crowd around me, but not obsessed with it either. There are some pretty strict rules in this club: no pictures, no video, all secrets. What happens in Slick's is supposed to stay in Slick's. But whatever. Worst case scenario, a video gets out – much like the one between Turner and Naomi – and the world knows that Lola and I are together. I'll just adopt my friend's attitude on that and say *fuck it*.

Lola reaches down and unbuttons my pants before I take over, pushing her hands away and wondering how the hell we're going to get away with this, dressed in jeans and all that. A skirt would've been a little easier. I smile against Lola's lips as I unzip her and crowd in closer, trying to hide her body with mine. To be fair, there are people on either side of us, engaged in pretty much the same fucking activity, but it doesn't matter. Lola is mine now.

I feel my lips twitch as that basic male urge washes over me. It's alright though, all good. I don't mind being Lola's too. I've been at this world too long to think that owning a woman is even possible, let alone that it means shit. A partnership – that's what this is all about.

"Bear with me," I growl around another wild kiss.

DOLL FACE

"Quickies with jeans take some serious skill." I push her jeans down her hips and let my mind fill with images from the parking garage, of pushing her knees back and fucking her on the hood of some random dude's car. My blood heats up in time with another one of Turner's screams. It echoes around the club, bouncing off the chandeliers and seriously fucking with my head. That's a million dollar shout right there. Apparently, quite literally, too.

I free my cock from my jeans, thanking the Gods above that Lola's new skinny jeans are some weird ass stretchy fabric and not straight up denim. That's a fuck of a lot harder to maneuver around. I spin Lola around and hold her close to me, letting her brace herself on the wall with her hands.

"It's gonna have to be from behind again, doll face. Hope that's okay with you?" Lola murmurs her approval, pushing her ass against me, as I slide my cock against her swollen wet folds, tasting that heat with the head of my cock, feeling an anxious jump in my pulse as I start to push inside of her. I have no way of knowing that I'm mirroring Turner's night with Naomi on that fateful Thursday night. Eh, even if I did, it wouldn't have changed anything anyway. At least for us, our night's not gearing up towards being nearly as gnarly as his.

I thrust deep, one quick stroke, just like that and fill Lola up with my cock. My lids flutter and my body spasms at the naked feel of her body against mine, her slick heat, the rough ridges of her pussy massaging my shaft as I move against her, almost uncontrollably. *Holy Christ on a Cracker.* How the fuck can you do something so many times and not think a thing of it, and then one day, everything just changes and something that was insignificant becomes *everything*?

"I want to get you pregnant, Lola," I whisper and she groans, shoving herself harder against me. I don't even know how she can hear me over the crush of the crowd as they cry for Turner, throw themselves at his feet. That's what it means to be a rock god, I guess. Even in your blackest moments, you have to be able to claim the audience, make them submit. I wonder if I'm in that category too now? Or if I'll ever be?

"Do it, Ronnie," she shouts back at me, not caring who's listening, not giving a fuck who might be watching. We slam our bodies together hard, harder, hardest. There's no love required for this slick oiled motion, this exchange of fluids. Yeah, sure, I love her, I do. One day soon, I'm going to just fucking say it. For right now, this works. This feels fucking *perfect.* I push Lola's sleeve up and squeeze her leopard tattoo. That's what she is

DOLL FACE

right now, like a wild cat. "Do it," she growls again, rocking against me, bringing me to orgasm a hell of a lot quicker than I'd like. I want to savor this moment, eat it up with a spoon and come back for more.

I let the drums in completely then, ignore the little technical errors or the other bullshit that bugs me, and just try to listen to the music. What they're playing right now is shit that *we* wrote after all. Even if the notes aren't perfect, it's still *ours*. Just the fact that these guys have memorized our shit, played it enough that they can whip it out at a moment's notice is impressive to me. I don't care about anything else.

I bite back the orgasm by clamping my teeth down on my tongue, slamming into Lola's ass as the crowd spins behind me, like a whirlpool, trying to pull us in and drown us in its depths.

The pummeling bite of the drums nips at my heels, spurring my hips faster, harder, deeper. Lola cries out and collapses forward, her body tightening, her fingers curling against the wall. If this really was a one-night stand right here, I know I'd be crawling back for more, begging for it, desperate for another taste of this woman.

I'm feeling good, letting my worries wash over and past me as I lose myself inside of Lola, loving her even as

I let myself devolve into an animalistic mass of muscles and cock and testosterone. Feeling *real* good until I spot Paulette Washington in the crowd not a dozen feet away from us. She's got a smile on her face, arms crossed over her plain black T-shirt. She might not be wearing a suit right now, but her blue jeans and neutral eyeshadow leave her just as invisible. *Crap.*

If I physically could've pulled myself away from Lola in that moment, I would've. But I can't. The pull between us is ten times as strong as the riptide that makes up the sweating, drooling, panting crowd. I growl out a curse and curl my fingers against her hips, spilling myself inside of her, relishing the moment at the same second I'm fucking *hating* Paulette Washington.

Lola moans, reaching a hand back and grasping for me like she's afraid I'm going to stop, and then she collapses, forcing me to grab her around the waist and drop us both to the floor. Sweat is pouring down her face and her lips are curved in a crooked half-smile.

"Fucking fuck, Ronnie," she whispers, looking over her shoulder with a contented expression of feminine possessiveness that makes my heart hammer. Unfortunately, when she sees my face, the expression drops away and she's shoving me back, yanking her pants back into place while I do the same. I help Lola to her

DOLL FACE

feet as she narrows her eyes at me and then follows a nod of my chin to the TV producer and her admittedly terrifying expression. There's a ... blankness ... there that I don't like, that leaves me really uneasy. *The hell is this?* "That bitch," Lola snorts, grabbing my hand and dragging me towards Paulette. I almost want to run in the other direction, but what good would that do me? Better to face this shit head on. "Interrupting my first raw dog with my new bloke. Motherfucker." I almost smile at Lola's slang, *almost*. But then I get close enough to Paulette to hear her voice when she speaks.

"Mr. McGuire," she says, her voice as pleasant as the hiss of a snake. Wonderful. A quick glance over my shoulder shows me that Turner's still onstage. Good. I look back at Paulette.

"What the fuck do you want? Something about the way you're staring at me tells me this isn't just a coincidence that I'm seeing you here tonight, is it? You must *really* want that reality show." Paulette laughs, her blindingly brilliant teeth reflecting back the throbbing club lights like a fireworks show inside her wide mouth.

"After what I just witnessed? Of course, I do. That's TV gold right there, Miss Saints, Mr. McGuire." She takes a step back, pushing her back against the dancers around her. I guess they sense some of the strangeness that I do and most of them move away without protest. "I was wondering if I could have a moment of your time?"

"The answer's no, Paulette. I don't know how to make that any clearer." Paulette keeps smiling at me. That's the scariest part of all of this. Still smiling. But there's something else about her tonight that kind of freaks me out, something that either wasn't there before or was very carefully hidden. That's when I see the dots of crimson on the back of her hand, like spots of red paint. Or blood. Could very well be blood, right?

Lola sees it too and we exchange a glance.

"Oh," she says, cringing and wiping the back of her hand on her shirt. "Silly me. Things got a little messier than I'd intended."

"What the fuck are you talking about?" I ask, and she sighs, sweeping pale strands of brunette over her shoulder. Her eyes slide past me, catch on Turner for a moment before she drops her gaze back to mine. I squeeze Lola's hand tighter, keep her fingers clenched in a death grip. I won't go through the shit I went through at the concert ever again. If Paulette has a gun, a knife, or what the fuck ever, I'm ready. At this point, I'm ready for just about everything. "What is going on here?"

"I'd like to talk elsewhere, Ronnie. There's just so, so

much I want to say," Paulette breathes with a sigh. "I was going to wait, try to stay patient with you, but there have been some … unforeseen circumstances that have arose that practically *demand* your immediate attention."

"Wow. I had no idea that reality TV was such a cutthroat business. Sorry if I don't seem more empathetic about the whole thing." Paulette laughs and shakes her head, looking down at the floor for a moment before running her tongue across her lower lip. She glances sharply up at me.

"Remember how I told you my sister fell prey to her addiction?" I raise an eyebrow. "Well, she wasn't addicted to any of the usual culprits. No drugs, no alcohol, not even power or money. She just … well, she was addicted to a man."

"I see," I say and exchange another look with Lola. Her blue eyes are open wide and locked on Paulette like she's just as sure as I am that something shitty is going to happen. Of course it is, right? I thought our roller coaster of crap had hit the top during the concert. I think I was right about that, but see, here's the thing, even after the roller coaster gets to the top, it's still sitting pretty high and there's a hell of a long way down that follows after. "And this has to do with us how?"

"Well," Paulette begins, sighing like I'm being difficult, "this really would've been easier in private." She shakes her head again and digs out a cigarette. Huh. Didn't peg her as a smoker. Guess we all have our little surprises. "Anyway, what I maybe should've told you right away was that my married name is Washington. Strange, right, that a modern woman like me would change her name to match her husband's? It's a long story, so I won't get into that." Paulette sucks in her lower lip with a pop and then pokes me in the chest with a finger. "It's just that my maiden name has a certain stigma attached to it." My heart picks up its pace, and I feel my throat going dry, constricting tight. *Oh no. No. No. This is over. It's over. It has to be over. Over, over, over.* But nothing is ever that easy, is it? "Maybe you'll recognize it?" She takes a dramatic pause, but that's okay because I've already figured out what she's going to say. "Harding. No? No bells? How about America? Does *that* remind you of anyone? Maybe of a woman that your best friend's girlfriend shot in the face?"

I feel the blood drain from my own face. My mind drifts to Brayden Ryker, of his warnings that the *family* was involved in all of this just as much as Stephen was. As America was. *Travis, damn it. I love you man, but couldn't you have knocked up a less crazy woman?* Shit.

DOLL FACE

"America Harding was my sister, and now she's dead. You're going to help make that up to me."

✘ ✘ ✘

Brayden Ryker is sitting on my bed when we get back to the house.

Seeing him lounging there in the weak light from the bedside lamp should probably surprise me, only it doesn't. I just sigh and move into the room, letting Lola stumble in behind me. After her admission, Paulette gave me a business card with her number on it and disappeared. I didn't ask about the blood. To be honest with you, I don't want to fucking know. I really, really don't. I already had Turner call the hospital to check on Naomi and Blair. Since they're all still alive, since we all made it back here in one piece, I don't fucking care whose blood that is.

So Lola and I had some more drinks and we had a really good fucking time.

Perfect.

And now there's this.

I stand there staring at the redheaded Irish muscleman on my bed and cross my arms over my chest.

"Should we ask how you got in here or are you going to volunteer that information up for our benefit?" Lola asks, and a pang of guilt shoots through my chest. Despite the fact that Brayden shot Poppet in the face, right there in front of all those people, his name isn't anywhere on the Internet. According to the news sources, an *unnamed security officer* took down Lola's sister. I keep meaning to tell her the truth, but I haven't found the right time. Shit. Life is just flyin' by, isn't it? I don't even know how to keep track anymore.

"I wanted to show you how inadequate your security detail was," he says, rising to his feet and looking between the two of us with a careful gaze, one that analyzes and breaks down the very soul. "I know you don't think very highly of me, but only because you don't know the whole truth. Sometimes, it's best to feign inadequacy and let the cards fall as they may."

"What the hell does that even mean?" I ask, closing my eyes and trying not to lose my shit. I really want to beat the crap out of someone. Should've taken Cohen Rose in the hospital. Might've gotten the crud beat out of

DOLL FACE

me from Brayden's men, but it would've been worth the adrenaline rush.

"It means that I warned you. I really did. All I can say is, you're on the families' radars. I knew you would be, especially with Tyler's fate so up in the air right now."

"Rada*rs*," I ask, emphasizing the plural. "So both families: Harding and Hammergren. Am I right?" Brayden shrugs his broad shoulders.

"They're fighting for custody of Tyler right now. Not because either side *really* cares, but they've been ... competitive for quite some time. It was sort of an unfortunate inevitability."

I grit my teeth and feel Lola's fingers brush my arm.

"That's my friend's fucking kid you're talking about there, not just some 'unfortunate inevitability'. Fuck you, dude." Brayden smiles sadly and nods his head.

"Aye. I know that better than anyone, trust me. Here's the deal I want to make with you. I think I can solve both of our problems, that of you and your friends and even Tyler. And mine ... of a more personal nature. But it's going to take your complete cooperation." Brayden pauses and takes a deep breath. "I think if we play the game right, I can even get you the kid, get Tyler for you, if that's what you want."

"No court's going to grant custody of Tyler to me or anyone else in this house," I spit, hating that that's the truth, hating that Travis' son is going to be raised by people capable of hiring snipers to shoot single moms. Fucking A.

"Who said anything about court?" Brayden asks, and I can't help but take note of the fact that Lola *isn't* in jail right now. That no police officers stand guard outside Naomi's hospital room, only Brayden's people. Hmm. I'm just some dumb fuck from suburbia. I don't know shit about shit. This is *way* over my head right now.

"Why are you coming to me?" I ask and Brayden laughs, shaking his head.

"Because you're the only sensible one in the group," he says with a smile. I sigh and open the bedroom door, holding it for Brayden so he can get the fuck out and leave us alone. All I want is to get my daughters back, to get to know Lola, to make fucking music. Instead, I get this. "I'll be out of your hair then, but I hope you'll call me when you're ready. Sooner rather than later would be advantageous for both of us."

Brayden pauses next to the door and watches Lola and me like he feels sorry for us. Not a good sign. Not a good fucking sign. To look at someone with pity, there

DOLL FACE

has to be tragedy that you see overlaid on top of their souls. I've had enough tragedy in my life. I stare right back and after a moment, Brayden chuckles and disappears down the stairs, the sound of his boots echoing loudly against the marble.

"What are we gonna do?" Lola asks, but I'm not sure if I have an answer for her. I wrap my arm around her waist and pull her close.

In the midst of the uncertainty and the confusion, Naomi Knox opens her eyes, and Cohen Rose breathes his last bloody breath. In our bathtub, no less.

Amen to fucking cliff-hangers.

To be continued...

Dear Reader,

I think the roller coaster's just started to tip, don't you? More questions, more answers, more rock 'n' roll. Thanks for taking this crazy ride with me.

Next up, Sydney and Dax in "Heart Broke". Poor Dax, right? Got the crap beat out of him by a tornado, got his dead mom shipped to the hotel, watched Hayden kill herself. This poor guy really needs a reason to go on. Y'think Trey's sister, Sydney, has it in her?

It will NOT be the last book in the series, but the one after it will be called "Get Hitched" and feature Turner and Naomi. Make of that what you will. ;)

Oh! And it will totally have a cliff-hanger. Love your faces, babes. Peace out.

~C.M.

Ready for another dose of effed the hell up?
Hard Rock Roots Book 8: "Heart Broke"

If you enjoyed "Doll Face", you might like the sexy southern biker boys of the "Triple M MC" series.

Losing Me, Finding You

C.M. STUNICH

CHAPTER 1
Amy

I wake to a dull roar that quickly becomes deafening. The sound rattles the windows in my bedroom and sends my father into a raging fury about those darn criminals which I can only assume refers to the motorcycle gangs that have been rolling into town lately for the antique bike show. My father does this every year, says these things every year. I should really move out.

"Amy," my mother says, opening my door the same way she has every day since I started kindergarten. "Time to get up. We're meeting your aunt over at the church to plan the potluck on Saturday." I smile and nod, hold my tongue and refuse to tell her that a potluck plans itself. People bring dishes; other people eat them. There isn't much to figure out.

"Thanks, Mom," I say and blow her a kiss as she backs away and resigns herself to listening to my father complain.

What he conveniently forgets is that those 'criminals' make up a pretty hefty portion of our town's summer economy. Without them, I don't think many of the shops downtown would still be in business. I sigh and stand up as another wave of noise approaches from the direction of the highway. Moved by my curiosity, I stand by the window and part the drapes so I can catch a glimpse of the men and women who are so far outside my realm of being that they might as well be aliens. They wear leather and have piercings and tattoos. The open road is their home and mine, mine is this three bedroom, two bath prison which is perfectly nice but so stifling that sometimes, it makes me sick.

I watch the wave of bikers drive by and press my fingertips to the shaking glass.

"Take me with you," I whisper as they fly by and disappear around the corner. I imagine what it would feel like to just run away with them, try something new, something different. I shake my head and turn away. It's not going to happen, not for me. Girls like me don't wrap their arms around men in leather, straddle massive hunks of metal that my mom refers to solely as death traps, drive to cities we've never been. Girls like me put on their yellow camisoles, their white sweaters and their below the knee skirts. We grab our purses, slather on some clear lip gloss and sit in the passenger seat while our mother talks about the nice boy who just moved to town with his parents. Poor guy, I think as I imagine his fate. He may as well have the words 'fresh meat' tattooed on his forehead like one of those biker boys. The girls from my church are going to be all over him. After all, in a town of five thousand people, it's not as if we have many choices. I should go to college, I think as my mom continues to talk in the background. Maybe somewhere far, far away. I sigh and smile at my mother who's patting my knee. Like I said, me, coward. Period.

"I'm so glad you're here!" my aunt says as she comes out the front doors of the church in an outfit disturbingly similar to mine. "We have a serious problem." She sighs and makes the sign of the cross which bothers my mom because we're not Catholic. My aunt loves church functions, church rummage sales and church gossip, but I don't think she really likes church in and of itself. I bet she'd be hard pressed to even remember Jesus' role in the whole of things. I'm not judging her, but I just think she's shallow and as see-through as a piece of glass. I'm like that, too, I think, but I wish I wasn't. I wish I had some substance.

I tune out my aunt and turn slightly, so I can see the main thoroughfare of the town down the hill from us. It's absolutely packed with people, humming with this wild energy that makes the hairs on my arms stand on end. I've never been to the motorcycle show which seems strange since I've lived here my whole life. My father, however, has always forbidden me to go. This year, even though I'm twenty-one years old, isn't any different. I really should put my foot down and let him know that I'm an adult and can make my own choices, thank you very much, but I haven't felt passionate enough about anything to take a stand.

When my mom and aunt start to move inside, I follow them and sit at the table with the other lunching ladies while they plan the same potluck we have every month, the one that doesn't really need any planning. Of course, under the table I have the greatest treat of all, one that doesn't involve church or yellow sweaters or cheese casseroles. Under the table, my book boyfriend is sucking on my toes.

"I want you like I've never wanted anyone else," Adam says to me as he kisses the arch of my foot and starts to move his way up my leg, ever so slowly, teasing my skin with his teeth, tasting my thighs with the hot heat of his mouth until he comes to my –

"Amy?" my mother says, waving her hand in front of my face. I look up and see seven curious expressions staring back at me.

"Hmm?" I close the book around my hand, determined to dive back in as soon as the setting permits; it's the only way I'll stay sane. The rest of the day isn't exactly looking up as we have plans to help my cousin try on wedding dresses. My mother wanted to wait until the motorcycle show was over, but Jodie's having a shotgun wedding (don't tell anyone outside the family, please) and she needs a dress like yesterday. The wedding is in two weeks after all, and there isn't much time left. My bridesmaid dress is going to be fuchsia. I know it is. I just know it.

"Can you make your caramel sticky buns for Saturday? The ones with the pecans?" Oh. Yes. Sticky buns. Maybe I can steal a few for myself, put them in my room and get ready for my hot date with Micah, the book boyfriend I haven't met yet but am absolutely thrilled to climb into bed with.

"Of course," I say with a smile as I tuck my chestnut hair behind my ear. It's the same color as the tabletop we're all sitting around. That's kind of depressing. The ladies go back to discussing the tablecloth colors and the chair arrangements in the dining room while I duck my head and reopen my book.

"Fuck me, Adam," I say as I turn over and put my ass in the air for his viewing pleasure. "Fuck me until the cows come home."

I snort with laughter and once again manage to draw attention to myself.

"Are you laughing at a book?" my mother asks, like that's so strange. I know she reads romance novels, too. She hides them from my dad under the sink in the bathroom and takes extra long showers so she can finish them. I shake my head and clear my throat.

"No, I just had a little something in my throat." I gesture vaguely around the area of my neck and try to keep smiling. I manage to divert their attention and make it out the door and into the car without further incident.

"I doubt we're going to be able to find a parking space," my mom says with a sigh as we wind down the road back into town, my aunt trailing too close behind us. "I may have to drop you off at the door so Jodie knows we're here. You know how moody your cousin's been lately." Yeah, I think, because she's like three months pregnant. I smile and try not to think about Adam's deliciously sexy body. I'm almost finished with him, so I brought along an extra. Daniel's ready and waiting inside my purse for me to finish these last few chapters.

"Okay, Mom," I say with a cheerful smile that quickly turns into an open mouthed gawp as we hit the first traffic light downtown and find ourselves in a sea of colorful characters that make little beads of sweat appear between my mother's eyebrows. "It's okay," I tell her before she starts to hyperventilate. "They're just people." My mother scoffs.

"Godless people," she says, and I don't correct her. There's no point. Some guy with a pentagram tattoo just walked by and much as I know that could mean anything, my mom thinks it's the sign of the Antichrist. "Do you have your pepper spray in your purse?" I took it out to accommodate Daniel, but I nod and tell her that yes, I do. I need an e-reader, I think as I imagine carrying thousands of books around in my hand. My father refuses to buy one for me, saying that digital devices like that are portals to hell in and of themselves. He let me have a computer, but he unplugs the Wi-Fi at night. I should really move out. "Go straight inside and don't talk to anyone."

"Okay, Mom."

"And please don't let Jodie try on anything that you know isn't going to fit. You know how moody she's been lately."

"Okay, Mom."

My mother pulls up to the curb and lets me out into the throng of people. I can see that she doesn't want to leave me there, but that she's more afraid of Jodie's wrath than she is of the motorcycle fanatics. I'd have to agree with that one. I start towards the front door of the bridal shop and then just stop. My mom isn't looking; Jodie doesn't know I'm here yet. Now's my chance to look around, just take a peek at the motorcycles. It won't take long; after all there's a whole row of them parked at the end of this block, just behind the red signs and yellow tape banning cars from this stretch of road. I glance over my shoulder to make sure that Mom's completed her U-turn and start down the sidewalk.

It's pretty obvious that I don't fit in here which is a strange feeling. I'm your typical, middle-class, all-American white girl with blue eyes and pale brown hair, but I'm the one that's drawing stares and raised eyebrows. Something about that is exciting to me, makes me hold my head high and strut like I'm something special. Instead of blending into the crowd, I'm standing out. Fantastic.

I pause next to a big, blue bike with metal that shimmers like the lake in summer, reflects the early afternoon sunshine into my face and makes me squint. I bend down to read the sign.

"You like Road Kings, beautiful?" a voice says from behind me, and I spin around to find a man standing far too close to my behind. My ass, I correct myself. You're an adult; you can say it.

"Um." My eyes are looking directly at a black T-shirt stretched over a wide chest, and I have to tilt my chin up to find the face of the man with the most amazing body ever. Oh. My. God. He looks just like my book boyfriend! "I, uh, it's pretty," I say which makes Mr. Motorcycle laugh.

"Pretty?" he says with some sort of Southern accent that I can't place. "I've never heard 'em described like that, but I guess you're right. She's one, hot fucking bitch."

"E-excuse me?" I say, floored by this man's language, and his fall of sandy blonde hair, his dark brown eyes that are even now sweeping my body like I'm one of the bikes for sale. He licks his lips and steps even closer to me. "S-she?" Mr. Motorcycle laughs again and I jump. I can't help myself. I've never been so close to a man, let alone one with a sleeve of tattoos and muscles that are slick and moist from the hot sun overhead.

"Can't very well be a he, right? The only thing I'm willing to ride cross country is a she." He winks at me, but I can't respond, not with him standing so close to me. My throat has just closed up and my mouth is dry.

"Um, okay," I say and my voice comes out in a whisper. The man, who has the most beautifully chiseled face I have ever seen, reaches out and brushes his fingers across my arm, making me shiver.

"If you like this baby, I could show you mine," he says and I have to blink several times before I can respond.

"Yours?"

"My ride, beautiful. You want to come see?"

"I ... " I see my mom come around the corner at the end of the block and reflexively reach out my hand for Mr. Motorcycle's massive bicep. My fingers curl around his hard flesh and my whole body goes up in flames. Oh. My romance novels suddenly make a whole lot more sense. My skin feels hot and flushed, like it could conduct electricity. I look up into his face and see that he's looking at me like he's the predator and I'm the prey. "I ... I have to go," I say as I step around him and start back down the block at an even quicker pace than I came.

"Hold up there," says the man with the dark eyes and the skulls on his upper arm. He grabs my wrist and spins me around. "You in town for the show?" he asks, as I clutch my purse against my chest and try not to pass out. It's awfully hot out here, and my pulse is thumping in my neck like a live thing.

"I live here," I whisper and he releases me with a wicked, nasty smile that gives me all sorts of strange feelings in my gut. "Why?"

"Well," he says with a glance over my shoulder. "I thought you might want to grab a drink or something?"

"Um." I steal a glance down the block and see that while my mom is gone, my aunt is staring at me like I'm possessed. Uh oh. "I have to go." I start to turn away, but he reaches out and grabs me by the arm, firm but not rough. I shiver.

"Come on, beautiful," he says. "Tell me your name."

"Amy," I say quietly, too quietly. "Amy Cross."

"Austin," he says, and that's it. "Now, Amy, I'm not letting you go until you promise to meet me back here tonight for a drink." I look into this man's dark eyes and feel like I'm falling and burning up at the same time. Two beautiful, beautiful ways to die.

My aunt is coming towards us now, and I can see that she's digging around in her purse. She's probably got her pepper spray in hand. Or a cross. I have to get out of here.

"I ... " Austin does not look like the kind of man that likes to hear the word no. "Okay," I say and he releases me with a smile.

"Yeah? Alright, maybe six?" I nod, just to get away from him, never intending on holding up my end of this one-sided bargain. "See you then, pretty girl."

I turn away and run all the way back to the bridal shop.

CHAPTER 2
Austin

"Who the hell was that?" Mireya asks me as she wraps her long fingers around my bicep and breathes her hot breath against my skin. I watch Amy's tight, little ass as she catches up to an old lady in a sun hat and starts to explain things with her hands. Why do girls like that always gesture so much? Beats the fuck out of me.

"Just some chick I asked out for drinks," I tell Mireya as I spin to face her and grasp her under the chin. She's exotic, dark haired, and feisty. She's also into things that have the ability to surprise even me.

"If you fuck her, can I watch?" Mireya asks as she wraps her arms around my waist and rubs her breasts against my chest, making me hard as a rock in the middle of the damn street. Or maybe that's because I'm still thinking of little Miss Amy with her sharp as shit blue eyes and her rounded body, bent over that bike, ass up in the air like she was waiting for it. I smile.

"Sure," I tell Mireya, taking hold of her hips and glaring at the guy down the block from us. He's checking out her ass, and it's pissing me off. What can I say? I'm a possessive motherfucker. "She might be a hard one to snag," I say although I'm fucking with Mireya a little. I don't just want to snag Amy. I want to own her.

"Why's that?" Mireya asks as she stands on her toes and kisses my neck. She's got on this perfume that doesn't fail to excite me, not even after all these years. Mireya and I go way back. I think she'd marry me if either of us were into that, but I'm not exactly the marrying type.

"I'll bet you a hundred bucks that she's a virgin," I say to her as I run my fingers through her dark hair and kiss her hard. She's got lips that could tame a cougar, that girl does. I pull away and grab Mireya by the hand. I might have a date with Amy tonight, but that doesn't mean I can't have a little fun with Mireya until then. "But I know you're not," I say, and she smiles at me, sharp lips curving up wickedly in the corners.

"Not unless you want me to be," she whispers, pulling my hand up to her hot mouth and biting my thumb gently. Mireya's dark eyes pull me in and wrap a web around me. She's off the chain fucking hot. No wonder she's always been my favorite little sugar. "If you're into innocent, little

Southern girls, I've got a pair of cowboy boots I could wear for you." She pauses. "With nothing else." I grin and pull her forward, wrapping my arm around her waist.

"Sounds good to me, beautiful," I say as she follows me obediently across the street and towards the doors to our hotel.

I can't say that I'm surprised when we're interrupted.

"You!" a voice shouts from down the street, and I turn to find the old lady in the yellow hat storming towards me, purse in one hand, a black can in the other. Goddamn it. I've been around long enough to know a can of pepper spray when I see one. Amy is scurrying along behind the woman with one hand shielding her face from the street and the other tugging at the woman's pink jacket. I drop my arm from Mireya's waist suddenly, like I'm afraid it'll scare Amy off. Shit, Austin, if the girl can't handle it, let her go. I keep my arm at my side.

"Yeah?" I ask as Mireya sighs and lights up, moving away from the scene of the crime and towards a pack of shirtless dudes that are hovering a little too close to her bike. She doesn't like to get involved in my altercations. Not to say that there are a lot, but I have been known to start some trouble. "Something wrong, gingersnap?" I ask the lady as she removes her hat and reveals a head of scruffy, orange curls. I'd have pegged her as Amy's mama, but there's no way these two are that closely related. Amy has that long, soft hair that's perfect for pullin'. When I see her glance up at me with a pained expression, I just want to reach out and wrap it around my fist, tug her to me and take those sexy lips between my teeth until she cries my name.

"Excuse me!" the old lady snorts as she waves the black can in my face. I don't flinch. These old Southern broads are tough as leather, and I am in no way ready to take on a lady whose blood runs with the fire of the sun and the earth, no ma'am. "But you need to keep your hands to yourself. If I see you touching my niece again, I might feel the need to call the sheriff and give him a piece of my mind. It's bad enough that we have to put up with your people year after year, but that doesn't give you the right to harass my family!" I take a deep breath and try to control my anger. If Old Lady Gingersnap had been a man, I'd have decked her. As things stand, she's a pretty old thing with firecracker eyes and a sharp tongue. A little respect can go a long way, provided it's applied in all the right places.

"You're right," I say to her, although my eyes are all for Amy. I don't think she knows how hot she looks in that little sweater. If it were up to me, I'd tear it right off her shoulders, slam her against this wall and show her a real good time. Amy looks like she's in need of some fun. Her neck is stiff and her eyes dart every which way, so she doesn't have to look at me. She isn't scared. Oh no, not this little lovely. She's excited. I can practically smell her excitement, her curiosity. This is a girl that's been dying to get out for awhile, and it's just a matter of time until she snaps. Maybe I could help her along a little? "I had no right to touch Miss Amy here. If you'll accept my deepest apologies." I reach out and grab Old Lady Gingersnap's hand, pressing it to my lips for a kiss. She blushes, but she doesn't spray me with her can which is a whole other sort of euphoric. There is nothing worse than getting sprayed in the face with that shit. "I'd like to make it up to poor Miss Amy by taking her out tonight."

"I already gave you my answer," Amy hisses as she drops her hand and takes a deep breath like she's preparing for trouble. Her blue eyes finally lock onto my face and hold my gaze without flinching. There's a whole lot more to sweet, little Amy than first meets the eye. She's telling me yes, but she's telling her auntie no. Smart girl. I'm not usually the type of guy that aunties approve of. They want to fuck me, maybe, but they don't approve. Nuh uh. "Come on, Megan," she says to her aunt who has finally tucked her pepper spray away with a sigh. "Let's go before Jodie has a fit." Amy starts to turn away, but she keeps her eyes on mine until the last possible second. When she finally tears them away, I have an almost physical reaction to chase after her. How fucking strange is that?

"First time I've seen you beat down by an old lady," Mireya says as she returns as quickly as she left. I wouldn't say she's the jealous type, but maybe she can tell that I like Amy. A lot. And I have no clue why.

"Well," I say as I pop a cigarette into my mouth and take Mireya into my arms. "You've never been up against an Old

Gingersnap like that. You're from up North, so you have no idea what these Southern ladies are like."

"Oh?" she asks as she leans in and kisses my neck. "And you don't think I'm a tough bitch? Why don't you let me prove it to you?" I tangle my fingers in her hair and pull her head back, so I can get a good look at her. Oh yeah. Mireya is hot, no doubt about it. Why the fuck then, am I thinking about Amy Cross when I start to kiss her?

ABOUT THE AUTHOR

C.M. Stunich is a self-admitted bibliophile with a love for exotic teas and a whole host of characters who live full time inside the strange, swirling vortex of her thoughts. Some folks might call this crazy, but Caitlin Morgan doesn't mind – especially considering she has to write biographies in the third person. Oh, and half the host of characters in her head are searing hot bad boys with dirty mouths and skillful hands (among other things). If being crazy means hanging out with them everyday, C.M. has decided to have herself committed.

She hates tapioca pudding, loves to binge on cheesy horror movies, and is a slave to many cats. When she's not vacuuming fur off of her couch, C.M. can be found with her nose buried in a book or her eyes glued to a computer screen. She's the author of over thirty novels – romance, new adult, fantasy, and young adult included. Please, come and join her inside her crazy. There's a heck of a lot to do there.

Oh, and Caitlin loves to chat (incessantly), so feel free to e-mail her, send her a Facebook message, or put up smoke signals. She's already looking forward to it.

www.cmstunich.com, www.facebook.com/cmstunichauthor, twitter.com/cmstunich, www.goodreads.com/cmstunich